The Mystery of the
Chinese Junk

"Don't wait for me!" he yelled, and hurled the line into
the water.

THE HARDY BOYS MYSTERY STORIES

THE MYSTERY OF THE CHINESE JUNK

By FRANKLIN W. DIXON

COLLINS · *London & Glasgow*

ISBN 0 00 160534 8
PRINTED AND MADE IN GREAT BRITAIN

CONTENTS

The Mystery
of the
Chinese Junk

·1·

Hong Kong Junk

"JOE, look out! That launch will hit you!" shouted Frank Hardy from the beach.

A split second before, his brother Joe had surfaced after a dive off a float. Now the launch was almost on top of him!

"That's Clams Dagget's boat!" Frank cried to two companions, Tony Prito and Biff Hooper. All stared ahead in horror.

A third boy, plump Chet Morton, who had been bobbing like a cork in the cool, blue water, had seen the oncoming launch and dived under the float with Joe Hardy. The craft roared off, the pilot paying no attention to the two swimmers. In a moment they came to the surface and swam ashore to join the others.

"Whew! That was close!" Chet gasped. "Thought I was a goner. Clams must be going blind!"

"He's as absent-minded as they come!" Joe stormed, panting.

"He sure is," Tony agreed. "I don't see why the town of Bayport lets him run a ferry service to Rocky Isle."

"Probably because no one else has a boat big enough or wants the job," Biff suggested.

Suddenly Frank grinned. "Maybe we fellows can run

9

a service of our own—in a Chinese junk from Hong Kong. I know where one is for sale cheap."

The dark-haired boy, a year older than his blond brother, said that their Chinese-American friend, Jim Foy, had told him only the day before about the boat.

"Jim's cousin lives in New York City," Frank explained, "and works as a salesman at a place in Staten Island where the junks are sold. New ones cost plenty, but the company isn't even advertising this secondhand boat. They're asking only a fraction of its original value."

"Say, that sounds great," Joe broke in. "And a ferry business would solve our summer work problem."

It was a bright June afternoon, a few days after Bayport High had closed for vacation. The five boys had gathered for a swim and to make plans for earning money during the next two months.

"You mean we'd charge passengers for picnic excursions to Rocky Isle?" Biff asked.

As Frank nodded, Tony remarked, "Good idea, if we could raise enough money to buy the junk, and provided it's seaworthy."

"It might have an interesting history," Frank said, not at all discouraged by Tony. "The junk may once have belonged to a Chinese pirate and have jade treasure hidden aboard!"

"How can we lose?" Biff declared with a grin.

"A real Chinese junk would be sure to attract attention here on Barmet Bay," Chet remarked.

The price of the junk was several hundred dollars, but after much calculating, all the boys except Chet decided that they could raise equal shares from their savings.

"Gosh, fellows, I'm sorry," said Chet. "But you know I've just bought all that spelunking equipment and I—"

Joe grinned. "You can take out your share in work," he said, whereupon the stout boy groaned. The last thing Chet ever wanted to do was work!

"It's more fun exploring caves than swabbing decks," he mumbled. "But I can put in fifty dollars. Who's going to make up the difference in the amount we need?"

"Jim Foy might, if he got a share of the profits," Tony suggested.

"Okay. What's stopping us?" said Joe eagerly. "Is it a deal?"

The five high school chums shook hands solemnly, then pulled on their jeans and shirts. It was decided that the boys would get their parents' permission for the trip first, then Frank would contact Jim Foy and ask him to telephone for an option to buy the secondhand junk from Hong Kong. If everything was in order, the boys would leave the next morning by bus for New York City.

Tony and Biff went off with Chet Morton in his fire-engine-red jalopy. Hopping into their own yellow convertible, the Hardys drove back to their pleasant, tree-shaded home at the corner of High and Elm Streets.

As Frank and Joe came in the kitchen door, they were greeted by Miss Gertrude Hardy, their father's tall, angular sister, who now lived with him and his family.

"Dinner will be on the table in a minute," Aunt Gertrude said, lifting a flaky steak pie from the oven.

"Mm! Does that smell good!" Joe exclaimed. "Double helping for me, please!"

"Same here!" Frank added, sniffing the delicious aroma.

"Never mind the flattery about the food." Miss Hardy waved them off, but Frank and Joe observed a pleased expression on her face. "It's a wonder this crust isn't burnt to a crisp with you two getting home so late," she scolded.

The boys, chuckling, went to wash their hands. Although their aunt was sometimes peppery in manner, the brothers were as fond of her as she was of them.

When they came to the table, Frank and Joe each found an extra-large serving on his plate and exchanged knowing grins. Aunt Gertrude poured milk into their glasses, then said with a sigh:

"Don't know what ails me today. I just seem to ache in all my joints."

"That's too bad, Aunty," Frank said sympathetically as he held her chair and she sat down. "You rest after dinner. Joe and I will wash the dishes."

"And break half of them most likely!" Miss Hardy retorted. But her face softened. "Still, it's a kind offer. I may accept."

As the brothers ate, they asked Aunt Gertrude if she had heard from their parents, who were now in California. Fenton Hardy, once a crack detective on the New York City police force, had retired to the thriving seaside town of Bayport, where clients from all over the country sought his services as a private investigator. At present, he was at work on a case in Los Angeles, seeking to track down an international thief known as the "Chameleon". Mrs Hardy had flown to the West Coast with her husband for a holiday.

"Your father," Aunt Gertrude replied, "phoned this afternoon. He said to tell you boys that if you want to help him out on this case, keep your eyes open for a pair of rare gold cuff links with a bluish amber tiger set in them. They've been reported stolen in Hong Kong and smuggled into this country. In your father's sleuthing he learned that the Chameleon, who collects priceless jewellery, is trying to get hold of such a pair. If you find them, you may also find the Chameleon."

"It sounds like hunting for a needle in a haystack," Frank remarked, "but if we should come across either the cuff links or the Chameleon, we'll certainly let Dad know."

Though amateur detectives, the brothers had solved many mysteries, and hoped to follow careers similar to that of their father. From *The Mystery of the Aztec Warrior* until their latest adventure in Canada, *The Viking Symbol Mystery*, Frank and Joe had experienced many exciting and dangerous adventures.

Suddenly Frank clapped a hand to his head. "Aunt Gertrude, I almost forgot. Joe and I have another project."

The brothers outlined their scheme for purchasing the Chinese junk. Then, with quickened pulses, they awaited Miss Hardy's reaction.

"Well," she said finally. "If it'll keep you boys occupied this summer, I guess it's all right. By the way, where is the money for your share coming from?"

"We have some in Dad's safe up in his study," Joe replied. "It's the reward money Frank and I got for solving a difficult case. A brand new one hundred-dollar bill for each of us."

Frank got up and hurried to the telephone. After learning that Biff, Tony and Chet were also set for the trip to buy the junk, Frank called Jim Foy. The Chinese-American boy was amazed to hear the proposal and excused himself for a few minutes to speak to his parents. Returning, he said:

"My parents say I may go. I will phone my cousin at once and have him place an option on the junk. When shall I meet you fellows?"

"Just before ten o'clock tomorrow. Bus terminal."

"I'll be there. This is a terrific break for me."

Frank returned to the table to find Joe urging his aunt to go to bed. She agreed, adding that she was disgusted with herself for not feeling as strong and vigorous as she generally did.

"Anything else we can do for you—besides wash the dishes?" Frank asked.

"Yes. Try to be quiet. Noise makes my head hurt. If you want to watch TV or do anything else, please go to the recreation room in the basement."

The brothers quickly washed the dishes, then went downstairs. They laid plans for the Staten Island trip, then Frank went to make a call to Chet Morton on the cellar extension.

Joe, meanwhile, hurried upstairs, dialled the combination on his father's safe, and opened it. While locating the money for the Chinese junk, he noticed a Manila packet marked *Secret File on Chameleon*.

The young sleuth took out the two crisp one-hundred-dollar bills with the picture of Benjamin Franklin on the face and Independence Hall on the back. Joe closed the safe and turned the tumblers. As he walked downstairs, he looked at the bills. Having worked on a counterfeit case, he knew a good deal about currency.

"Federal reserve notes, one from the eighth district, St Louis, and the other from the fifth, Richmond," he mused, noticing the green seal, and the letters H before one serial number and E in front of the second. "And what do you know? This one starts with H18 and ends with F. Hmm. *Hardy—Frank*—eighteen years old."

Joe studied the second bill. "And this one begins E1015 and ends with A. E for Elm Street on our corner." He chuckled. "And JO are the tenth and fifteenth letters in the alphabet! That means me. The A—well, that could be for Aunt Gertrude."

Joe went to his mother's desk in the living room and obtained an envelope printed with the Hardy name and address. He slipped the bills inside. Just then, Joe thought he heard a car stop in front of the house. Laying the envelope on the mantelpiece, he went to look out of the window. No car was in sight. "Guess I was wrong," Joe told himself and hurried down to the basement.

Ten minutes later, just as Frank finished the conversation with Chet on the phone, he suddenly gasped and pointed to one of the basement windows. A fearsome-looking Oriental face was pressed against the pane —the man's teeth bared in an evil grimace!

For a moment the boys were too startled to act. Before they could make a move, the lights went out, plunging the basement into darkness!

"A prowler!" Joe exclaimed. "And we forgot to turn

on the alarm!" The warning system automatically rang a bell in the house and floodlighted the Hardy grounds when anyone approached.

"Too late now," Frank said. "Let's get that man! I'll go out the cellar door. You run upstairs and find out if everything's okay."

The boys dashed to the landing and Frank hurried outside. Joe continued to the top of the steps and put his hand on the doorknob.

"It's locked!" he murmured, rattling the knob and pounding on the door panel.

After a few tense moments Joe heard slippered feet enter the kitchen. Then Aunt Gertrude unlocked and opened the door.

"Mercy, what's all the racket about?"

"Someone locked us in after turning off the switch here in the kitchen," Joe explained. He pointed to the wall button, which was in the *Off* position. "You didn't—"

"Of course not," Aunt Gertrude replied tartly. "There must be a burglar in the house!"

"A burglar!" Joe echoed. The next second he raced into the living-room and stared at the mantelpiece.

The envelope containing the two new hundred-dollar bills was gone!

· 2 ·

Mysterious Engine Trouble

JOE, sure the burglar had made his escape from the house, dashed to the front door. He switched on the porch light. Out on the lawn he could see two figures struggling on the ground. One was Frank.

Before Joe could reach his brother, he recognized the other fighter. "Jim Foy!" he cried out.

The two boys separated and grinned sheepishly.

"Gee, I didn't mean to scare you guys so much that you'd tackle me," Jim said, panting.

"You mean that was *you* staring at us through the basement window?" Frank exclaimed.

Jim nodded. He screwed his face into a horrible grimace. "The Oriental Avenger—that's me!"

Frank laughed, but Joe said quickly, "Jim, we've been robbed! Frank, our two hundred dollars are gone!"

Frank looked amazed, and Jim said, "Fellows, I saw a man run out your back door, just after the cellar light went out."

"Let's hunt for him!" Joe urged.

The trio made a quick search of the grounds and adjoining streets, but the thief had eluded them.

"Did you get a look at him?" Joe asked Jim.

"Not a good one. It was too dark in the yard. The guy was tall and thin. Say, come to think of it, he made no noise. Probably was carrying his shoes."

"So there won't be anything but sock footprints," Frank commented. He went for a flashlight and found this to be the case. They were of no use in identifying the thief.

The searchers returned to the house. Aunt Gertrude had checked to find out what the burglar might have taken and how he had entered the house. She had found a cut in a screen at an open window, but reported nothing missing. Joe now told her about the stolen money.

Miss Hardy sucked in her breath. "Two hundred dollars!" she cried out. "Joe, why did you leave it on the mantelpiece? Go and tell the police right away. But you'll never get those bills back. Money's too hard to trace." Then, seeing the crestfallen look on her nephew's face, she added, "Never mind. I'll lend you boys two hundred dollars for your share in buying the junk. You can repay me from your profits."

Frank and Joe relaxed, gave their aunt a tremendous hug, then urged her to go back to bed. "I'll turn on the prowler alarm," Frank told her, and immediately went to do this.

Meanwhile, Joe had picked up the phone and was giving Police Chief Collig, an old friend of the Hardys, a report on the stolen money, including the letters and first few serial numbers on the bills.

"Good clues, Joe," the officer said. "I'll send out word right away."

When the excitement subsided, Jim Foy informed the

brothers he had come to tell them that he could not go to New York after all. "So I brought you my share of the money for the junk," he explained, pulling several bills from a pocket.

"Too bad you can't go," said Joe. "By the way, what is your cousin's address in New York?"

"He lives in Chinatown with his parents. My uncle Dan Foy owns a restaurant there called the Canton Palace." Jim wrote down the address and telephone number and handed the paper to Joe.

The next morning, before Frank and Joe were dressed, the prowler alarm sounded, then the front doorbell began to ring persistently.

"Who can that be?" Frank asked, puzzled.

He slipped on a dressing-gown and hurried downstairs with Joe at his heels. When Frank opened the door, he found himself face to face with Clams Dagget. The wiry, stooped old pilot thrust his way inside. As usual, he was wearing a striped jersey, jeans, and a squashed-down yachting cap.

Joe said, "Clams, if you've come to apologize about nearly running me down yesterday—"

"Apologize!" Clams roared in a hoarse voice. "Nothin' to apologize for. Now listen. I heard that pal o' yours, Biff Hooper, talkin' on the dock last night about how you fellers are buyin' a Chinese junk and startin' a passenger service to Rocky Isle!"

"What about it?" Frank asked coolly.

"It's a blamed outrage! Takin' bread out o' an old man's mouth, cuttin' in on my business! I won't stand for it!"

"Now just a minute," Frank said. "No one's trying

to take away your business. There'll be plenty for both our boats."

"What do *you* know about it?" Clams shook his fist at the Hardys. "I'm warning you young snips you won't get away with this!"

Suddenly a voice behind them called, "How dare you threaten my nephews!" Aunt Gertrude, coming from the kitchen, bore down indignantly on the visitor.

Clams stepped backward. Aunt Gertrude pressed her advantage by inching him out of the house and closing the door. Then she put her hand to her head.

"I—I feel faint. I'd better lie down."

Joe helped his aunt to the living-room couch, while Frank rushed off to get her some tea. As she sipped it, her nephews ate the breakfast she had prepared. Presently Miss Hardy declared that she was feeling fine again. Nevertheless, the boys insisted that she relax while they washed the dishes.

"Aunt Gertrude, promise me you'll call a doctor if you don't feel well," Frank urged, when the brothers were ready to leave.

"I promise." Miss Hardy then handed Frank a cheque for two hundred dollars. "You can cash it on your way to the bus," she said.

Both boys thanked her and gave their aunt resounding kisses on the cheek. Then they drove downtown, and after cashing Aunt Gertrude's cheque, went to the Bayport bus terminal. Frank left the car in an adjoining car park. Chet, Biff, and Tony were waiting for them.

"Hi, fellows!" they exchanged greetings. Ten minutes later their bus pulled out.

They rolled at a fast clip through the countryside, but

it was late afternoon before the travellers reached New York.

"What's first on the schedule?" Biff asked as they paused in the terminal waiting-room.

Frank suggested that they book in to a hotel, then do some night sight-seeing. He telephoned the Canton Palace but learned that neither Jim's uncle nor cousin would be there during the evening, so the boys decided not to go to Chinatown. Instead they strolled along Broadway, and were fascinated by the crowded theatre district, with its huge neon signs, restaurants and hotels.

The next morning the boys checked out of their hotel and took an early ferry to Staten Island. A short bus ride along the waterfront brought them to the pier where the Hong Kong Trading Company had its warehouse and office.

"Hey, look! There they are!" Tony exclaimed.

Two of the Chinese junks were tied up at the dockside, while three more could be seen resting in cradles inside the warehouse, with their masts unstepped. The five boys entered the office.

"Something I can do for you?" a bald-headed man asked, rising from his desk.

"We've come to see about the secondhand junk," Frank told him. "Is Mr Foy in?"

"I'll get him."

Ben Foy was a pleasant-faced young man. He gave the callers a friendly smile and said he was sorry that Jim had not been able to come.

"I'll show you the junk you took the option on," Ben said. "I think it's a good buy."

Even with its sails furled, the craft had a romantic,

adventuresome look. The boys tingled with excitement as they jumped aboard. The junk was a thirty-foot two-master, carrying two large sails and a jib. Amidships there was a round-roofed cabin.

"Boy! What a dream boat!" Joe exclaimed.

"It's the biggest, most seaworthy craft you can get for the money," Ben Foy boasted. "These jobs are shipped by freighter from Hong King. Normally we just sell new craft. This used one got into our consignment by mistake, so we're letting it go at a sacrifice."

He added that the junk was built of Borneo ironwood with one-inch-thick mahogany deck planking. "It'll last for years."

"Look at that figurehead up front!" Biff exclaimed. Leaning over the prow, he pointed to the painted figure of a stern-looking, slant-eyed Chinese mandarin holding a scroll in his hands.

"What are those eyes up at the bow?" Tony asked. He pointed to two realistic-looking eyes, made of glass, one on each side of the prow.

Ben Foy laughed. "'*Boat with no eyes cannot see!*' That's an old proverb," he explained.

Other decorations, such as Oriental dragons and banners, were painted in bright colours at various points around the junk. At the stern was the name *Hai Hau*.

"That's Chinese for 'Queen of the Sea'," Ben Foy translated.

He showed the boys the junk's equipment, which included awnings to cover the afterdeck in bad weather, a *euloh* or sweep oar, to assist the ship in light wind or against the current, and a thirty-five-horsepower auxiliary outboard engine.

"Part of the stern area can be used as galley space," Ben added. "Here's a charcoal stove, and there's a small refrigerator compartment in the portside locker."

"That's for Chet!" Tony laughed.

The boys were highly satisfied and declared they were ready to purchase the junk. In answer to questions from Frank and Joe, Ben gave them a number of tips on handling and sailing the craft. Then they all went into the company's sales office to sign the purchase papers.

"Before sailing the junk home," Ben said, "you'll have to go to the Coast Guard office and obtain a Certificate of Inspection."

"How long will that take?" Frank asked.

"It could be several days."

At this announcement the boys sighed. "Say, what's going on outside?" Biff asked suddenly.

Through the open window they could see four Chinese gesturing as they examined the *Hai Hau*. A moment later the men crowded into the office. One was tall, the others short. All had cruel, calculating expressions.

"We wish to buy the *Hai Hau*," the tall Oriental declared. He took out a bulging wallet.

"Sorry." Ben shook his head. "You're too late to buy that junk. But we have some brand-new ones which I can show you."

The tall man snarled, "I said we wish to buy the *Hai Hau*—that is the one we prefer!"

"Well, you're out of luck. These fellows have just purchased it."

The four Chinese glared at the youths and burst into

angry chattering, but Ben repeated firmly that the deal was closed. He finally managed to usher the obnoxious men outside.

Chet looked worried. "Why do you think they only wanted our boat?" he asked.

"Yes. Why?" Tony echoed. "It wasn't advertised. This could mean trouble for us."

"Oh, stop worrying," Biff scoffed. "They may have seen it being unloaded here."

The boys went to the Coast Guard office, and told an assistant what they wanted. He asked them to sit down and wait.

Half an hour went by. One hour. The boys fidgeted and walked around.

"We may have to sit here for days," Chet said aloud following his statement with a loud groan. The other boys looked glum.

A commander, standing nearby, overheard Chet's remark. With a smile he walked over and said, "Boys, I think we can take care of you now."

All of them jumped up. He laughed and said, "One will do—the one with the receipt for the purchase of the junk." Frank followed him and in a short time the transaction was finished. The boys hurried off. They ate lunch, then stowed their gear and some food aboard the *Hai Hau*. Frank revved the motor and they shoved off.

"Good junking!" Ben Foy waved a smiling farewell from the pier.

It was a hot, dead-calm day, so there was no point in hoisting the sails. They travelled southwards along the Staten Island shoreline. Biff handled the tiller while Frank studied a chart on which he had plotted their course. Part of the homeward trip would be along inland waterways.

"Hey, the engine's missing!" Joe exclaimed suddenly.

"Sounds like the plugs are fouled," Tony said.

"Maybe it's the oil film from storage."

Before the boys could check, the outboard began to cough and vibrate alarmingly.

"That's more than just the plugs!" Frank declared. He switched off the engine hastily and Tony removed the cowling. As Frank had predicted, the ignition system was not at fault. Evidently the trouble was more serious.

Chet groaned. "And Ben Foy guaranteed the engine!"

"So how do we get back to port?" Tony asked. "No wind, no sail."

"Use the sweep oar, I guess," Frank replied gloomily.

The boys unshipped the long, heavy euloh and fitted it on to the stern peg. Each of the chums took turns working as oarsman. At first they found the euloh clumsy to handle, but after a little practice they were able to keep the junk moving steadily.

The water was dotted with vessels moving through the Narrows, in and out of New York Harbour. Gulls screeched and wheeled overhead. Presently the *Hai Hau* returned to the Staten Island pier. After tying up, the boys hurried to inform Ben Foy of their plight. He frowned with surprise, but upon checking the motor himself, promised to have a new engine installed immediately.

"We'll live up to our guarantee," he assured the boys. "But it beats me what made that motor conk out! We overhauled it completely." Ben Foy said that he was leaving the office shortly but would give orders to have the work done. "If you boys decide to stay over, come to the Canton Palace as my guests," he urged.

As the Bayport group waited for a new engine to be installed, the four Chinese who had tried to buy the junk suddenly appeared at the dock. "For Pete's sake, why are they here again?" Tony muttered.

The tall leader walked up to the boys and offered to buy the junk from them at a price far higher than they had paid. Frank, as spokesman for his group, refused, but the Chinese and his friends continued to pester the youths.

"No deal—that's final!" Frank said.

The Orientals exploded into angry phrases in their native language but finally walked away. Chet said under his breath, "What's eating those guys, anyway?"

"I wish I knew," Frank replied, puzzled.

By the time the new engine was installed, it was too late in the day to start for Bayport. They decided to leave the junk moored at the pier and sleep on it overnight.

Tony, feeling uneasy about the safety of the junk if left unguarded, offered to stay aboard while the others visited the Canton Palace in Chinatown. "Those mystery men may even come back here and help themselves to it!"

Biff, Chet and the Hardys took the ferry to Manhattan. Alighting at the Battery, they asked directions from a policeman. Frank suggested they walk to the restaurant.

"Suit's me!" Chet said. Joe and Biff nodded.

Dusk was shadowing the city when they reached the outskirts of Chinatown. Presently Joe gave his brother a nudge.

"Don't look now, but I think we're being followed! Probably by those four guys who want the *Hai Hau*!"

· 3 ·

Shadowy Attackers

FRANK sneaked a swift glance over his shoulder. The men were coming up behind the boys, hats pulled low over their faces.

"Let's go faster!" Frank hissed. "Then we can find out if they're really following us."

The boys quickened their pace and turned at the next corner.

"They're still with us!" Joe reported.

Unfortunately, there was no policeman in sight; only pedestrians, who were, in the main, Orientals.

"We'd better shake those men off!" Frank decided.

The four youths broke into a sprint, ducking in and out among the sidewalk strollers. The pace got hotter as the pursuit continued. The boys cut through an alley, crossed a street, and turned at the next corner. For several minutes they dodged and doubled back through the narrow streets. Finally they were sure they had shaken their pursuers.

"Man, I'm bushed!" Chet panted as they paused for breath in front of a Chinese grocery. Then his expression changed. "Hey, look at all this chow!"

He pointed to the store window. Shark fins, pressed ducks, and dried squid were displayed along with Chinese herbs and vegetables.

"Interesting," said Frank, "but we'd better find the Canton Palace before those men spot us again!"

By this time, bright neon-lit signs were blinking on all over the neighbourhood, many in Chinese. Store windows were crammed with Oriental merchandise, including carved Buddhas, jade trinkets, and Chinese silk pyjamas.

"Here's the restaurant!" Joe exclaimed presently.

When they entered the dimly lighted restaurant, the headwaiter came forward and with a polite smile showed them to a booth. Frank asked for Jim Foy's uncle and cousin.

"Ah, yes, I bring them right away," the headwaiter promised.

A few moments later Mr Dan Foy approached. He was a pleasant, round-faced man with gold-rimmed spectacles. He said that Ben had had to go on an errand.

"You are friends of my esteemed nephew, I understand."

"That's right, sir." Frank introduced himself, Joe, and their two chums. "Jim is a good friend and he's one of our partners in buying the junk."

"So happy to hear that."

Mr Foy chatted with the boys a while and took personal charge of ordering their dinner. Soon the four youths were enjoying bird's-nest soup, roast duck, egg rolls, and almond cakes.

Suddenly a deep singsong voice said, "I understand you are owners of a junk called the *Hai Hau*."

The boys looked up, startled. The speaker was a giant Chinese, with a long melon-shaped head and jutting ears. He had glided out of the shadows to their booth.

"How do you know that?" Frank asked sharply.

"Did you not say so to honourable restaurant owner?" The man smiled. "Allow me to introduce myself. My name is Chin Gok. I would like to buy the *Hai Hau*."

"I'm sorry, but the boat is not for sale."

The huge Chinese smiled. "Do not decide too hastily. I will pay much more than it cost. Let us say, a profit of one hundred dollars?"

Frank glanced at the others, then shook his head. "No, thanks. We're keeping the junk."

Chin Gok's face went pale with rage, but he did not speak. Bowing, he walked away.

"Wow! A hundred bucks' profit!" Biff muttered. "Maybe we should have taken it!"

"Nothing doing," Joe declared in a whisper. "If that junk is so valuable, we're hanging on to it."

Worried by the strange events of the afternoon and evening, the boys were anxious to get back to the *Hai Hau*. They finished their meal, thanked Mr Foy for his hospitality, and left the restaurant.

"Let's take a taxi," Chet suggested nervously.

"Good idea, if we can find one," Frank said.

The boys hurried towards Chatham Square. As they passed a darkened doorway, Joe heard a shuffling noise. Before he could turn, someone grabbed him.

"Look out!" Joe yelled to the others.

The boys whirled to find themselves facing four masked assailants! The assault had come so suddenly there was no time to plan a defence. Fists swung wildly in the darkness as the youths fought off their attackers.

Bam! Frank landed a terrific right that sent one thug

reeling back against the wall. Biff was swinging like a windmill, while Chet's beefy strength was slowly wearing down another opponent.

Joe, whose arms had been pinioned from the back, was having the roughest time of all. But he fought tigerishly, kicking his opponent's legs.

Suddenly one of the masked men barked out something in Chinese. The boys assumed it was a warning that a policeman was coming, for they saw one in the distance. The next moment all four attackers went racing down a nearby alley in the darkness.

"Let 'em go," Frank advised as the others started after the thugs. "This might even be a trap."

"Those sneaking rats!" Biff panted. "I wonder if they were the same guys who were following us? And what's the big idea, anyhow?"

"Maybe this'll prove something," Joe said. He picked up a torn piece of newspaper. "When I was scrapping with that guy who jumped me, this fell out of his pocket."

"Let's see."

Frank held the paper up to the light from a nearby store. It was printed in Chinese.

"What good'll that do us?" Chet asked. "None of us can read Chinese."

"Mr Foy can. Let's go back and ask him," Frank suggested.

The boys retraced their steps to the restaurant. Mr Foy was shocked to hear about the attack. He took the boys into a back room and read the article to them in English.

It was a story about a smuggling plot, which had

just been uncovered by the United States customs authorities. It stated that while Chin Gok was a suspect, nothing had been definitely proved against him and he had been released.

"What's his game now?" Biff puzzled. "I mean, where does the junk come in?"

Frank frowned thoughtfully. "Remember, Ben Foy told us that the *Hai Hau* had been shipped to his company by mistake. Actually, it might have been a put-up job. Chin Gok may have used it to smuggle contraband into this country."

Chet's eyes bulged. "You mean there was treasure hidden aboard and not by some old pirate either?"

Frank nodded. "That would explain why all these guys are so eager to get hold of our boat. It's full of nooks and crannies where it would be easy for a smuggler to sneak stuff through customs."

Joe shot his brother a worried glance. If the *Hai Hau* did contain contraband, the boys might find themselves in real trouble. But neither of the Hardys wished to alarm their chums by pointing this out.

"Perhaps it would be safer if I called a taxi to take you back to the ferry," Mr Foy suggested. The boys agreed to this, and the restaurant owner added, "Please be careful!"

The chums arrived at the pier on Staten Island without further incident. Tony reported that nothing had happened while they were gone, and listened to their night's adventures with keen interest.

"Let's get away from here early," he urged.

The next morning, as the boys prepared to embark for Bayport a little after six o'clock, a short, slender Chinese man approached them on the pier.

"Good grief, another one?" Chet muttered.

Their visitor was dapperly dressed in a summer suit and straw hat. "Good morning, boys. May I introduce myself? George Ti-Ming. The *Hai Hau* is most pleasing to me. It is exactly like one owned by my family in China. I was disappointed to learn that you young gentlemen had purchased it, because I should like to have it. Perhaps you would be willing to sell for a suitable price?"

The boys exchanged suspicious glances. Was he another member of a large gang determined to get the boat, or were there three separate groups interested in it? And why?

"We do not wish to sell," Frank told Mr Ti-Ming.

The man shrugged. "There is an old Chinese saying that bad luck follows those who will not be reasonable. You may regret your decision."

The youthful owners of the *Hai Hau* began to suspect the same thing. But they rejected any thought of giving up the junk, and cast off as George Ti-Ming stood watching them, his eyes slitted with annoyance.

The sky was overcast, with a brisk breeze chopping up the grey-green sea. The Bayport crew hoisted sail to take advantage of the wind.

"Boy, at last we get a chance to enjoy ourselves!" Chet lolled back in the stern, lacing his hands behind his head.

"You said it," Frank agreed. "But we'd better keep an eye on the weather."

The outer harbour was alive with shipping, but gradually they left this scene of activity behind. As the *Hai*

Hau proceeded along during the late afternoon, the wind gradually died down and mist gathered over the water. Sails flapping, the junk had to depend on its motor.

"That fog's building up," Tony remarked. "We'd better hug the shoreline."

Joe, who was handling the tiller, nodded. "Looks as though it's going to be a real pea-souper." He cut speed as the fog became thicker.

The hooting of foghorns reached their ears. Frank began sounding their own power whistle, a blast every minute. Bit by bit, the fog closed in. Soon they were blanketed by a thick curtain.

"Think we should drop anchor?" Joe asked.

His question was answered as they felt a sudden bump from the bottom. The engine churned uselessly.

"We're aground!" Biff exclaimed.

Joe cut the outboard hastily, hoping that no damage had occurred.

"N-now what?" said Chet nervously.

Frank shrugged. "Wait it out till the fog lifts. It's about all we can do."

It was an eerie sensation, lying still on the water, cut off from the outside world. The boys took turns ringing the junk's bell. From time to time, muffled sounds drifted through the swirling mist.

Chet had taken charge of the galley. As he prepared to heat up cans of beans for supper on the charcoal stove, he accidentally spilled several red-hot embers on to the wooden deck.

"Watch it!" Tony yelled.

Joe doused the embers with a splash of water. "Take it easy, Chet!"

"This junk must be jinxed!" Biff grumbled.

The fog did not lift until morning. Biff and Tony pried the junk loose with the euloh oar and a boat hook, while Frank reversed the engine. Fortunately, no damage had occurred.

The boys resumed their voyage, making good time. They slept on board again that night and at midday on Saturday, triumphantly sailed into Bayport Harbour. A crowd gathered as the junk approached the main pier.

"Boy, look at the reception!" Chet exulted.

"All we need is a brass band," Tony agreed with a pleased grin. "This'll get our boat business off to a flying start!"

The boys' satisfaction dimmed considerably when they found themselves greeted by laughs and joking comments. Clams Dagget was in the forefront of the crowd, spurring on the spectators with jeering remarks.

"Here comes the 'Hee Haw'! I told you they was buyin' a real *junk*!" he hooted. "I'd sooner put to sea in a bathtub!"

Joe scrambled up on the jetty, ready to blast Clams angrily. But Frank laid a restraining hand on his brother's arm.

"Let him have his little joke." Calling out to Clams, he said, "It's pronounced 'Hay How'."

After arranging for space at a jetty that had day and night guards, the chums left the *Hai Hau* tied up, planning to get in touch with one another by phone. Frank and Joe hurried home. They found Aunt Gertrude pale and upset.

"I'm glad you're back!" she said, as they each gave her a hug. "There was a prowler here again last night!"

· 4 ·

Chet's Dilemma

"A PROWLER!" Frank echoed. "What happened, Aunt Gertrude?"

"The alarm bell went off in the middle of the night," Miss Hardy reported. "I jumped out of bed and looked down at the lawn. The floodlights were on and I could see a man dart off through the bushes!"

"What did he look like?" Frank asked.

"I could only see his back, but he seemed tall. Fortunately, all the doors were bolted." Upset by the recollection, Miss Hardy sank into an arm-chair. "Gave me a dreadful fright! I thought for a while I might faint!"

"Not a brave person like you!" Joe patted her shoulder affectionately. "Did you call the police?"

His aunt sniffed. "Certainly not! What good would that have done? The man was gone."

After fixing lunch for the boys, Aunt Gertrude went upstairs to lie down. Frank and Joe ate with zest, discussing the case between mouthfuls of tomato soup, cold roast chicken, and angel cake.

"If that prowler was tall, he might have been the same guy who stole our two hundred dollars," Joe conjectured.

Frank nodded. "Sounds that way. We'd better report it to Chief Collig. I'd like to know if he has any leads on the thief."

"Afraid not, boys," the officer said. "It's my opinion the burglar has left town. But your report, Frank, sheds a new light on the matter."

After putting down the phone, Frank got paper and pencil and jotted down four objectives for him and Joe to accomplish. From their father, the boys had learned that thinking with a pencil often helped to clarify a case. Joe grinned wryly as he read what his brother had written:

1. *Find out who the prowler is.*
2. *Solve the mystery behind the* Hai Hau.
3. *Learn more about Chin Gok, George Ti-Ming, and the other four Chinese.*
4. *Get going with our boat business!*

"I'd say we have our hands full!"

"Ditto!" Frank agreed. "First, let's check the grounds."

The brothers looked around the house for footprints, but the prowler seemed to have left none, although the soil was soft.

"If you're looking for that prowler's marks, it's no use," Aunt Gertrude informed them from an upstairs window. "It rained here last night."

Frank and Joe spent the rest of the afternoon replacing the old alarm system with a new type to warn of anyone approaching. They tore out the wiring in the shrubbery and substituted an electric-eye "snooper-scope" arrangement, as Joe dubbed it. Next, the boys disconnected the outdoor floodlights and the shrill alarm bell in the house. Instead, they hooked up a series of buzzers on all floors. By this setup, the Hardys hoped to lure intruders close enough to be captured, rather than frighten them away.

"It should do the trick if that thief pays us another visit," Frank said when the job was finished.

"There's only one thing I wish we'd done differently; fix the system so that it would work with the doors open," said Joe. "But it's too late to change it. We must remember to keep them closed."

Remembering that they had not yet reported to Jim Foy, Frank telephoned him. The Chinese-American lad was thrilled to hear he was part owner of the *Hai Hau* but mystified by the boys' strange adventures on the Staten Island pier and in Chinatown.

"Is there any way your uncle or cousin could help us check up on George Ti-Ming?" Frank asked.

"Sure," Jim replied. "Uncle Dan's a member of the Chinese Benevolent Association. It has information on everybody connected with Chinatown. I'll ask him to find out."

"Swell!"

Before hanging up, Frank told Jim the brothers would meet him at the *Hai Hau* after church the next morning. The three gathered at twelve-thirty and Jim's eyes sparkled as he walked round the junk.

"She's a beauty," he said enthusiastically. "I guess she's pretty old, but in good shape. When do we begin business?"

"As soon as we find out what the law requires to carry passengers," Frank replied.

On Monday morning, when the Hardys were eating

breakfast, Tony Prito stopped by in one of his father's construction company's pickup trucks.

"Hey, you know my cousin Ralph who's a Coast Guard officer?" Tony said. "Well, I got all the info from him yesterday about operating a passenger boat for hire."

"Great. What is it?" Frank asked.

"Well, we can't carry more than six passengers without going to a lot of trouble in keeping to regulations."

"That's okay," said Joe cheerfully. "We'll make two or three return trips each day."

"Frank," Tony went on, "you and I will have to get pilot's licences."

"What about the rest of us?" Joe put in.

"Can't. You have to be eighteen."

"What's involved in getting the licences?" Frank inquired of Tony.

"A written test and a physical exam by our family doctors or the Public Health Service," Tony replied. "Bring along a letter from your doctor."

"Okay, I'll make an appointment this morning. What's the test on?"

"Navigation laws—and first aid, fire prevention, buoys, sanitation, etc."

"You fellows had better pass or we won't be in business," Joe warned with a grin. Frank winked at Tony and clutched his stomach. "Oh, I've developed a horrible pain. Afraid I have appendicitis."

"Too bad," said Tony. He got up from the chair on which he had been sitting and limped across the room. "No use, Joe. Can't run a junk with a bad leg."

"Okay, you guys." Joe laughed. "Get going!"

Frank promised to meet Tony on the *Hai Hau*'s jetty at two o'clock and called the Hardys' family doctor, Dr Bates, as soon as Tony had left. The brothers spent the next hour composing an advertisement announcing their boat business, to be turned in at the Bayport *Times* office as soon as the licences to run the *Hai Hau* were granted.

The doctor's nurse had given Frank an appointment at one o'clock sharp. After getting his checkup and a letter from Dr Bates reporting a perfect score, Frank drove to the pier. Tony was already there and reported that he too had been given a clean bill of health. He showed Frank several life jackets.

"Ralph advised me to get these," Tony said. "We can split the cost later. Did you read up on your rules and regulations, Frank?"

"Sure did. I think I know 'em okay."

Frank and Tony went off to the Coast Guard inspector's office, and passed the written test without any trouble. The boys were given papers showing they had licences to operate the *Hai Hau*. They then parted and Frank drove to the Hardy home.

"Now we can run the advertisement," said Joe, relieved. He and Frank took it to the newspaper office.

"What's next?" Joe asked.

Frank suggested that the brothers inform their other partners they were now ready for business. "Let's start with Chet."

He drove the car to the Morton farm on the outskirts of Bayport. Only Chet's mother was at home. She said that Chet had gone to practise something to do with spelunking at the abandoned Tyler farm, a mile down the road.

"I didn't know that place had a cave in it," Joe remarked as he and Frank drove off.

Frank pulled into the rutted dirt drive of the Tyler farm and stopped in front of the weatherbeaten, deserted house. The boys got out.

"Hey, Chet!" Joe shouted, cupping his hands.

The brothers began scouting the fields, which were overgrown with weeds and brush.

Suddenly a shrill whistle came as if from nowhere, followed by a ghostly voice calling, *"Hey, you guys! Help!"*

"It's Chet!" Frank exclaimed. "Where is he?"

A further search revealed an old dry well. Attached at the top of the well to a tree was a broken length of rope. At the bottom of the gloomy shaft they could make out the round face of their chum looking up at them pitifully.

"For Pete's sake, what happened?" Joe called down. "You all right?"

"Yes, I'm all right, but get me out of here!"

Joe ran back to the car and returned with a rope. After much tugging and hauling, the Hardys finally succeeded in pulling Chet to safety.

"Thanks, fellows!" he panted.

The Hardys eyed in amazement the strange-looking garb of their friend, who was perspiring heavily.

"Good grief!" Joe burst out laughing. "What're you dressed up for—a moon flight?"

The stout youth was wearing large, one-piece green overalls. They fitted snugly at wrists and ankles, and had leather patches at the knees and shoulders. The opening at the neck revealed two heavy, red-check woollen shirts underneath, which made Chet's oversize figure bulge more than ever. Cotton working gloves, huge hiking boots with thick socks, and a hard hat topped with a miner's lamp completed Chet's costume.

He also carried a police whistle on a lanyard around his neck, a waterproof plastic bag over one shoulder, and a length of nylon rope wrapped around his plump midriff.

"All that in this weather?" Frank shook his head. "Heat must've gone to your brain, Chet."

"You just don't know about spelunking," Chet defended himself, adding proudly, "The name comes from the Latin word for cave, *spelunca*."

"Do you need this much gear for exploring caves?" Joe put in.

"Sure, it's dangerous. You have to be prepared for emergencies," Chet replied.

He opened his shoulder bag and took out a compass, a special watertight flashlight with a plastic lens, extra bulbs, batteries, matches, and candles in a small waterproof container. There were also plastic reflecting tape, several strips of which he had already pasted on his helmet, a cigar-shaped first-aid kit, a small knife, extra carbide and a repair kit for the lamp, and two canteens.

"One holds drinking water and the other extra water for the lamp," Chet explained.

The Hardys stared at the heaped-up assortment. Chet beamed with pride as he stuffed the various objects into his kit bag.

"If all that equipment's for exploring caves," said Joe, "what were you doing inside the well?"

Chet reddened slightly. "Well—uh—I thought I'd try chimneying. That's a way of climbing up a narrow passage by pushing your feet against the opposite side and inching up. I let myself down by the rope and it broke. Then when I tried to chimney up, I found the well was too wide. So there I was. Good thing I heard you guys talking."

Joe grinned. "And it's a good thing our rescue rope didn't break. You put enough of a strain on it yourself, without adding that ton of hardware you're carrying!"

Chet was undaunted. "Go ahead, laugh. Spelunkers find some terrific sights underground."

"I'll bet it is interesting," Frank conceded. "Maybe we can all take a crack at cave exploring this fall after our Chinese junk trips are over."

"Now you're talking!" Chet exclaimed. "There are some swell caves right around Bayport."

Frank then told him about getting the licence and running the advertisement. "Tomorrow let's take the *Hai Hau* on a trial run round Barmet Bay and over to Rocky Isle," he suggested. "We can figure out how much it's going to cost us, so we'll know what to charge our passengers."

Chet hesitated. "I have promised to take a couple of people spelunking," he said, grinning mysteriously. "Thought you fellows might even come along. I didn't know you'd be ready to start our ferry service so soon. I'll come if I can, but don't wait for me."

"Okay."

The Hardys took Chet home, then drove to their own

house. The brothers found Aunt Gertrude entertaining a club friend, Mrs Witherspoon, a widow. They greeted her, then went in to the kitchen for lemonade and biscuits.

Mrs Witherspoon had a piercing voice, and the boys could plainly hear the conversation. ". . . must tell you, Gertrude, about the most wonderful new doctor who's just opened an office here in Bayport! Dr Montrose, his name is."

"Indeed? What is he like?" Aunt Gertrude asked.

"Simply amazing! He's already helped Cora with her sciatica, and Mrs Pritchard says he's calmed her nerves no end. You ought to try him." Mrs Witherspoon went on to say that the wealthy Dr Montrose also advised his patients in financial deals. He had already sent several women to a stockbroker friend of his to make investments.

After the visitor had left, Aunt Gertrude came into the kitchen to prepare dinner.

"Humph!" she said. "It's my opinion that fellow Montrose is a fraud! Probably every women patient— and they're all widows—will lose her money! I think it's my duty to expose him."

"You'll need proof," Frank reminded her.

"Then I'll *get* proof!" Miss Hardy declared. "I'll turn detective and ask him here to treat me. I'll soon find out what he's up to!"

· 5 ·

A Strange Warning

THAT evening Frank and Joe went over their list of equipment on the *Hai Hau*. "Guess nothing's missing," said Joe.

At that moment Frank snapped his fingers. "Something very important is missing," he said. "Our junk has no short-wave radio, and we might need one to get in touch with the Coast Guard. Let's fix up that portable set in the basement."

"You mean the one Dad just took out of the old car he sold—the set with the Coast Guard, the police, and the Hardy frequencies on it?"

Frank nodded. Two years ago the boys' father had had a two-way set rigged up in their basement, so that he could have quick communication not only with the Bayport police, but with the cars of his sons and his detective Sam Radley.

"Swell idea!" said Joe. "Let's get started."

The brothers worked until nearly midnight getting the portable set ready for the *Hai Hau*. Then, yawning, they climbed the stairs to bed.

Early the next morning Aunt Gertrude telephoned Dr Montrose and asked him to call at the house. He arrived before nine o'clock, just as the boys were ready to leave. Mrs Witherspoon was with him.

"I was in the doctor's office, Gertrude, when you phoned," the widow explained, "so I thought I'd come along and introduce you two. Believe me, you can have every faith in Dr Montrose!"

The doctor smiled confidently. He was tall and thin, with a small head perched on a long stringy neck. His eyes were sharp and piercing.

"And these are Miss Hardy's nephews, Frank and Joe," Mrs Witherspoon went on.

The boys shook hands, then said they were about to leave the house for several hours.

"Mrs Witherspoon, would you be able to stay here and answer the door or phone while my aunt is consulting Dr Montrose?" Frank requested. He did not like the idea of leaving Miss Hardy alone on her detective mission!

"Oh, I'll keep house while the doctor's here," Mrs Witherspoon promised good-naturedly.

Frank and Joe thanked her. Before starting off Joe hurried to the basement to turn on the short-wave set.

"I'd like to call Aunt Gertrude later and hear what she found out from that 'stock swindler'," Joe confided to his brother as they hurried to the dock. Frank grinned.

At the pier the Hardys found Biff and Tony polishing woodwork on the *Hai Hau*. Frank and Joe pitched in to help them. A few minutes later Jim Foy showed up.

"Welcome aboard, honoured guest," Joe said solemnly, bowing low in Oriental manner.

The Chinese-American lad chuckled. "That's corny enough for a Grade D movie about China! Which reminds me, I wrote to my uncle about George Ti-Ming."

"Fine," said Frank. "Let us know as soon as you hear anything."

Jim Foy scrambled down from the pier to join the others. Frank reminded them of the Chinese newspaper item concerning Chin Gok and the smuggling plot. "Let's search this junk and see if anything's still hidden aboard."

"Right!" Tony agreed.

The boys began a search of every crack and crevice. They were about to give up when Joe gave a shout from the bow.

"Hey, someone bring a screw driver!"

Frank grabbed one from the tool locker and hurried to join his brother in the bow. The other boys watched as Joe carefully pried loose a tiny silvery object which had become wedged between two deck planks.

"What is it?" Biff asked, staring with wide-eyed interest. Then he exclaimed, "A bullet!"

"Good grief!" said Tony. "I wonder when that missed someone and landed here!"

Frank and Joe examined the bullet. "My guess is that it came from quite a distance," Frank said. "Probably a stray intended for a practice target."

"I hope you're right," Biff said with an uncomfortable feeling.

Tony urged that they stop searching and set sail. But the Hardys told Biff and Tony they needed time to install the two-way radio set they had brought along.

"I figured we could use it for ship-to-shore communication with that radio setup in our basement," Frank explained, "and also call the Coast Guard if we need to."

The job of installing the short-wave equipment was soon completed. Tony started the outboard and they pulled away from the dock. Once clear, the sails were hoisted and the centre-board lowered.

"Wind on the port beam," Frank observed.

Soon they were scudding over the water at a brisk clip. It was a bright sunny day and Rocky Isle was clearly outlined on the horizon beyond the mouth of Barmet Bay.

"Let's try calling Aunt Gertrude," Joe suggested presently. "Over an hour has gone by since Dr Montrose came to the house. I'd like to know how she made out with her detective work." Speaking into the mike, he said, "Hardy boys to Elm Street. Come in, please!"

There was no response, except a faint sputter of static. Repeated calls were not answered.

"Aunt Gertrude must have gone out," said Joe.

Suddenly a hissing voice broke in, "Hardys, I warn you. Do not sail the *Hai Hau*!"

The boys were electrified. "Good grief! Where did that come from?" Tony exclaimed. "Your house?"

Frank became grim. "If it did, that voice might have been a prowler's. Aunt Gertrude may have run into trouble!"

"You're right," said Joe. "We'd better get back there pronto!"

The *Hai Hau* was turned in a wide sweep, then headed back to Bayport. Biff tried to ease the Hardys' worries by suggesting that the warning had not come from the boys' home after all. "Someone who knows your frequency may just be teasing you," he said.

Frank and Joe were not convinced and listened carefully for any further message. Halfway back through the bay, Joe gave the radio call signal again. To everyone's amazement a familiar voice crackled over the junk's speaker.

"Hi, fellows! This is Chet Spelunker!"

"Chet! For Pete's sake, where are you operating from?" Joe cried out.

"Your place," the stout boy replied. "The front door was open, so I walked in. Hope you don't mind. Just then I heard your signal and hustled down to the basement."

Joe asked, "Were you the wise guy who sent us that warning before?"

"What warning? What are you talking about?"

Chet was dumbfounded when he heard of the mysterious threat received over the junk's radio. "It sure wasn't my voice you heard—I just got here," he said. "I only stopped by to—well, to see if your aunt had any spare cake for a picnic."

"Where's Aunt Gertrude?" Joe asked.

"She's not here, worse luck. I guess she must be out. Didn't answer when I called her," Chet replied.

"And no one else is there?"

"Not a soul. And the house looks okay." Chet chuckled. "About that picnic. Callie and Iola are going on the spelunking trip with me."

Callie Shaw, an attractive blonde, was Frank's favourite date. The couple usually double-dated with Iola and Joe.

"Some guys have all the luck," Joe remarked.

"Well, see you later!" Chet called. "I'll close the door."

The plump youth signed off, leaving Frank and Joe more mystified than ever. Where was Miss Hardy? Who had left the door open? And who had sent the strange radio threat, and from where?

Biff spoke up. "Since everything is okay at your house, Frank and Joe, let's continue our trip to Rocky Isle."

The Hardys agreed, though they would have preferred going home to be sure nothing had happened. Once more the junk was turned and the boys tacked out of the bay and emerged on to the open sea. Rocky Isle lay about five miles ahead. The northern end of the small island was a tumbled mass of rock, rising to a sheer cliff, on which stood a white lighthouse. The southern portion of the land was flat and sandy. The only home on it, which was near the shore, was occupied by the park-keeper, Dave Roberts.

"Might be a good idea to practise landing at the public wharf," Frank suggested.

Tony laughed. "You mean we'd better look good when we bring our first load of passengers?"

The wind continued while they crossed the stretch of open water. As they neared the southern end of the island and approached the boat landing-stage, Frank told Biff to stop the engine.

"Let's try it under sail," he said.

Frank swung the junk's nose into the wind to lose headway and ordered the others to slacken off on the sheets. As they did, the wind shifted. A sudden gust sent the junk straight towards the quay!

"We'll crash!" Jim cried.

Acting quickly, Joe shoved the fenders over the side,

grabbed a bamboo boat hook, and staved off the shock of impact. With a creaking *scrunch* the junk swung into position alongside the stone pier!

"Whew! Let's not do *that* again!" he gasped.

"Nice going, boy!" Tony clapped Joe on the back. "With you aboard, what is there to worry about?"

The boys practised several more landings, both with and without the engine. All went off smoothly. Satisfied, they headed back towards Barmet Bay.

Two miles from the island, a motorboat came racing up astern and pulled alongside the junk. Aboard were two men in Coast Guard uniforms. One, wearing the insignia of a chief petty officer, hailed them in a loud voice.

"Heave to! We're coming aboard!"

· 6 ·

Coastal Search

THE boys aboard the *Hai Hau* were surprised at the unexpected order. The Coast Guard officer's scowling manner hinted at trouble.

"Anything wrong?" Frank called across the water as Tony stopped the outboard.

"We're checking on all private craft in the Bayport area!" the man shouted back. "That junk isn't properly documented and you're subject to a fine. The *Hai Hau* will have to be taken back to the base in tow!"

Biff reddened angrily. "What do you mean? We have everything that is required."

"We got our Certificate of Inspection in New York," Tony called.

"Tell that to the warrant officer!" the man retorted. "We're still taking you in! You'll have to prove what you're saying."

He poised in the stern, ready to leap aboard the junk as his mate steered closer to the *Hai Hau*.

"Wait a second!" Joe ordered. With sharp eyes he had looked over the other craft. "That's no Coast Guard boat you're in," he said. "Where's your official ensign?"

The burly pilot's expression became ugly. "Don't get smart with us, kid! We'll ask the questions!"

52

"I'll bet they're phonies!" Frank cried out.

The men heard him. "Shut up or we'll clap you all in irons!" one threatened. As the boats touched sides, he vaulted over the gunwale.

Joe greeted him with a stiff-hand jab before the man could find solid footing on the *Hai Hau*'s deck. Taken off balance, he toppled backwards into the water. He came up spluttering and cursing. The helmsman shouted dire threats at the boys.

"Now's our chance!" Joe yelled. "Give 'er the gun, Tony!" He threw the helm hard over.

Tony revved the outboard and the junk spurted away from the motorboat. Its helmsman was too concerned with rescuing his partner to give chase.

Biff chuckled and pumped Joe's hand. "Nice going, pal!"

The boys hooted with laughter as they watched the man in the water being hauled into the motorboat, drenched and dripping. He looked balefully at the boys.

"You won't get away with this!"

His angry bellow carried across the water. He and his pal made no attempt to go after the boys, evidently realizing that they stood little chance against the *Hai Hau*'s husky and determined crew.

"Wow! This is more excitement than I bargained for!" Jim Foy said. "Are you fellows sure those guys weren't real coastguards from the Bayport station?"

"We'll soon find out!" Biff declared.

He warmed up the transmitter again and tuned in to the Coast Guard station frequency. All of the crew were much relieved when the base's radio operator assured them that no harbour patrol boats had been ordered to pick up unregistered craft. He also said that the officer in charge would send out a launch at once to hunt for the troublemakers.

"I wonder where those fakers got their uniforms?" Tony mused.

Frank shrugged. "Stole them probably. What I'd like to know is why everyone's so anxious to get hold of this junk."

"Maybe all the guys we've had run-ins with are members of the same gang," Joe conjectured.

Biff offered another theory. He suggested that the two fake coastguards might be cronies of Clams Dagget. "Maybe Clams hired them to keep us from starting our boat business," Biff said. "You told us, Frank, that he was angry when he came to your house."

"That's right."

The *Hai Hau* returned to Bayport without further incident, and was tied up at the pier. Jim Foy said he had to leave as he had a job to do for his father. The other four boys remained for a while, talking over their plans. Tomorrow was to be the opening day of their passenger service to Rocky Isle.

"Let's keep our fingers crossed!" Tony said with a grin as the meeting broke up.

"Don't worry," Frank replied confidently. "I'll bet we get a full boatload at every trip!"

Biff and Tony, who had chores to attend to, drove off in Biff's jeep. "See you tomorrow, fellows!"

"What'll we do now?" Joe asked his brother.

"Let's grab a hamburger," Frank said. "I'm starved."

"So am I. But first I want to phone the Coast Guard

and find out if they've picked up those two fakers."

The brothers went into a nearby restaurant which had a public telephone and made the call. The two men had not been caught.

As the Hardys perched themselves on stools, Joe suggested, "What say you and I try to trace those phoney coastguards? Maybe we can spot their boat. After all, we got a good look at it."

"Smart idea! We'll take the *Sleuth*."

The boys finished their hamburgers and hurried to the boathouse where they kept their motorboat. Minutes later, they were cruising along the shore of Barmet Bay. They went the full length of the three miles, first inspecting the north side, then the south. There was no sign of the craft anywhere.

"Let's try the ocean," Frank urged.

Leaving the harbour mouth, the Hardys turned northward along the coast. The ocean was as quiet as a pond. From time to time the brothers hailed fishing boats and other small craft to inquire about the motorboat. None of the skippers they questioned had sighted it, and the boys did not spot the craft hidden anywhere along the rocky, indented shoreline.

"Looks as if we're out of luck," Joe grumbled.

Frank was keeping binoculars trained along the coast. "Let's try south of the bay," he suggested.

"Okay. Let's go!" Joe swung the *Sleuth* round, leaving a frothing wake.

As it passed Rocky Isle to starboard, a small cabin cruiser crossed their bow. The man at the wheel waved to them. Frank shouted a description of the motorboat and asked if he had seen it.

"Sure, about ten minutes ago," the yachtsman called back. "Heading over that way!"

He indicated a sandy stretch of beach half a mile beyond the harbour mouth.

"Thanks!" The boys waved back.

"A break at last!" Joe muttered. He increased speed and the *Sleuth* lunged ahead, its bow lifting clear of the water.

As they neared the beach which the yachtsman had pointed out, the boys switched places. Frank took the wheel.

"Hey, this is where Clams Dagget lives!" Joe remembered suddenly. He trained the binoculars on the shore, picking out Dagget's shack. "Frank!" he yelled excitedly. "I see those two men who pretended to be coastguards. They're standing at the front of the shack, talking to Clams!"

Frank turned the motorboat towards the shore. As it beached in the shallow water of an inlet the boys leaped out and ran towards the shack.

At that instant their quarry sighted them. Breaking off the conversation with Clams, the two men dashed into the tall bulrushes behind the shack.

"After those fakers!" Joe shouted to Frank.

The marshy ground sloped upwards into scrubby underbrush, willows, and sumac. Frank and Joe could hear the men plunging forward, but soon lost sight of them. The boys were finally forced to give up.

"What luck!" Joe growled. "We almost had 'em!"

"Let's see what Clams has to say about them," Frank suggested grimly.

Dagget was lounging at the front of his shack, whittling

a piece of wood. He appeared unconcerned as the two boys walked up to him.

"Who were those guys?" Frank demanded.

"What guys?"

"The ones we were chasing."

Clams shrugged. "How should I know?" He began whistling airily as he continued work with his penknife.

"You'd better think hard!" Frank warned him. "Those fellows are—"

He broke off as an engine roared in the distance. A second later the boys saw their quarry's motorboat race from a nearby cove. It headed northward.

Joe clenched his fists in futile rage. "No hope of catching them with that kind of a start! But I can notify the authorities on the *Sleuth*'s radio. Wait here," he told Frank, and dashed back to the motorboat.

The young detective pressed the button for the Coast Guard frequency. He reported having seen the impersonators and that they had taken a northerly route in their escape.

Meanwhile, Frank had been questioning Clams Dagget. When he found him unwilling to talk, Frank flushed with anger.

"Listen, Clams—I'm warning you. Those two guys you were talking to just committed a federal offence."

"What!"

The old beachcomber's mouth dropped open in a look of alarm.

"You heard me. They're impersonating members of the United States Coast Guard. What's more, they tried to board our junk and take over," Frank added. "That could be attempted piracy."

"I don't know nothin' about 'em," Clams Dagget whined. "Never even seen 'em before. That's the truth!"

"Then what were you talking to them about? You were sure acting chummy!"

"They said they wanted me to do a job for 'em," Clams replied. "I don't know what. You and your brother came along and scared 'em off before they got a chance to explain."

Presently Joe returned and questioned Clams further, but finally both boys decided he was telling the truth. Boarding the *Sleuth*, they returned to Bayport.

It was almost seven o'clock when Frank and Joe arrived home. They found a note from Aunt Gertrude on the hall table. It said:

> *I feel much better and am going out. Dr Montrose is a good doctor. He did not talk about stocks and I had no chance to bring up the subject.*
>
> *Phone Chet Morton's mother as soon as you get in. She has phoned twice.*

Frank frowned. "I wonder what's up?"

He dialled the Morton's number. A woman's voice answered almost immediately.

"This is Frank Hardy, Mrs Morton. I—"

"Oh, thank goodness you got my message!" Mrs Morton sounded frantic. "Chet and the two girls haven't returned from their cave trip! They were due back hours ago! Please help us to find them!"

· 7 ·

Missing Spelunkers

FRANK tried to calm Chet's excited mother. "I'm sure there's nothing to be alarmed about, Mrs Morton," he said soothingly. "Joe and I will start looking right away. Did Chet tell you where he and Callie and Iola were going?"

"That's just it—he didn't say exactly!" Mrs Morton replied. "He did mention taking the West Road, but I don't know where. Oh dear, I never should have let them go!"

"Please don't worry," Frank said. "We'll find them."

As he hung up, Joe flashed him a questioning look. "What's wrong?"

"Chet and the girls are missing. Come on! We'll have to work fast before it gets too dark!"

The boys dashed out to their convertible and sped through the outskirts of town. Frank took the West Road. Outside Bayport, the road ran through a stretch of barren, rocky hillsides.

"Slow down," Joe said as they came to a junction. "Let's check this road. There might be a cave near here."

Frank braked the convertible and swung off on to the

59

unpaved road. Joe leaped out, hoping to find the tyre tracks of Chet's jalopy. He came back a moment later, shaking his head.

"No luck."

Most of the area was uncultivated, with scraggy brush and timber growing up the hillsides. As the boys drove along they passed a rock quarry and several gravel pits. Here and there, dirt lanes branched off, leading to scattered farms or other roads.

The Hardys checked several of these rutted paths. On the fifth try, Joe shouted:

"Hey! This may be it!"

Frank hurried to join him. His brother pointed out a set of narrow tyre tracks with a worn, old-fashioned tread pattern.

"Those are Chet's, all right!" Frank confirmed. "I noticed the treads that time we helped him change one of his tyres."

Hurrying back to their car, the boys turned up the lane. The convertible bounced and jolted so badly that Frank changed into low gear.

Moments later, Joe gave a cry of relief. Chet's red jalopy was parked ahead. It had been pulled off the lane into a bordering clump of poplars. Beyond the trees, the ground rose steeply.

"There must be a cave entrance nearby," said Frank. "We'd better take our flashlights."

Joe grabbed them from the glove compartment and the brothers hopped out. Daylight was fading, but a clear trail of crushed undergrowth plainly showed which direction the spelunkers had taken.

The brush finally thinned out amid tumbled rocks

and boulders. A few minutes' search, however, revealed an opening in the hillside.

Joe cupped his hands and yelled into the yawning darkness. "Hey, Chet! . . . Iola!"

No answer.

"Let's go in!" Frank urged. "The cave probably runs in a long way. They can't hear us."

Crouching, the boys entered. Once inside, they were able to straighten up. Frank and Joe stabbed the darkness with their flashlights. The yellow glow revealed a fair-sized cavern, at least thirty feet in width. Straight ahead, the darkness closed in again beyond the range of their flashlight beams.

"It's deep, all right," Joe muttered.

The boys pressed forward. Eventually the cave narrowed, then forked in two directions. The right-hand opening dwindled into a crawlway of pitch blackness. The left-hand fork, though a cramped tunnel, was high enough for a person to walk through.

"Which way?" Joe asked, hesitating. The floor of the cave was too hard to show footprints.

"Let's go left," Frank decided. "Chet and the girls probably took the easiest route if they'd never explored here before."

Joe nodded. "I sure can't see how Chet could squirm through a hole that size," he added with a nervous chuckle, gazing at the small opening.

Frank went first. The tunnel sloped downwards, and gradually broadened out.

"There they are! But—oh!"

Frank's cry was wrought with fear. A few yards

ahead, Iola, Callie and Chet lay motionless on the floor of a small, dead-end chamber!

The Hardys ran forward and anxiously bent over their three overall-clad friends. To the boys' relief, all were still breathing.

"What happened to 'em?" Joe asked, bewildered.

"Passed out, I guess. We must revive them!"

"We could use more light," said Joe. "But we ought to save our batteries."

Chet's carbide lamp was empty of water. Rather than waste time refilling it, Joe lit a candle taken from the stout youth's kit bag. As the chamber brightened with the soft glow of candlelight, Frank and Joe began reviving the trio. They chafed their wrists and bathed their faces with water from Chet's canteen. Presently Iola moaned, and the other two showed signs of regaining consciousness.

"Whew! I'm getting a headache," Joe sighed.

"Same here."

As the boys paused, they realized that their eyesight was becoming affected. Vision grew blurred and they began to pant.

"Joe, this place is short of oxygen and that candle's burning up what's left!" Frank gasped. "We must get out of here—fast!"

Frank lifted Callie to her feet and Joe did the same with Iola. The girls' knees buckled.

"Be simpler to carry 'em!" Joe said.

"Okay, but we'll have to speed it up fast!"

Frank swung Callie over one shoulder, while Joe picked up Iola. Nightmarish moments followed as the brothers wormed their way back through the tunnel to the mouth of the outer cave. Perspiring and panting, the boys gulped in lungfuls of fresh air, as they placed the girls on the grass. Then they hurried back to the dead-end chamber.

With lightning speed they gathered up Chet's spelunking equipment, stuffing most of it into their pockets. Then Frank put his hands under Chet's shoulders while Joe grabbed the stout boy's legs. Each held his flashlight clamped under one arm.

"Man! Chet—must weigh three hundred pounds!" Joe gasped out.

By the time the rescue mission was completed, Frank and Joe were so woozy from the bad air that they were nearing collapse themselves. Both dropped to the ground to catch their breath. In a few minutes Chet and the girls had revived enough to be able to tell their story.

"I knew we shouldn't stay in that dead-end cubby-hole too long," Chet moaned. "But when we started to come out through the tunnel, we heard some men talking, so we stopped."

The Hardys looked puzzled, and Joe asked, "Is that any reason for asphyxiating yourselves?"

"Wait'll you hear the rest!" Chet said. "They were talking about you two!"

"That's right!" Iola chimed in. "We heard one of them say, 'We'll have to take care of those Hardy boys before they spoil everything!'"

"They sounded plenty tough, too!" Chet said. He added plaintively, "I sure wish you guys wouldn't get mixed up in mysteries!"

Frank and Joe exchanged troubled glances. "What else did they say?" Frank asked.

Chet shrugged. "Don't know. They talked too low, but they started to come in farther. So we figured it would be safer to lie low till the men were gone, and we went back to the inner chamber. Then we blacked out."

Callie, who was trying to smooth her rumpled hair, flashed a grateful smile at Frank. "We'd still be there— and maybe dead by this time—if it hadn't been for you Hardys. Thanks a million for saving us!"

"She means you, naturally," Joe quipped to his brother. Then he blushed as Iola said:

"Well, I think *you're* wonderful, too! So there!" To back up her words, Iola planted a quick kiss on Joe's cheek, which left him gulping in surprise.

Before leaving the area, the Hardys decided to look for any clues that might lead to the men whom the spelunkers had overheard. They checked the ground carefully outside the cave and found several sets of men's footprints which differed from their own and Chet's.

"And notice this. The prints leading away from the cave are deeper than the ones leading towards it," Frank observed.

Joe nodded with keen interest. "You're right. Those guys must have been carrying something pretty heavy!"

"We didn't see anything in the cave when we entered," Chet spoke up.

"Which means," said Frank, "that it must have been taken out some time before you came—probably only a little while before."

"Oh!" Callie caught her breath. "You mean we just missed meeting those awful men!"

The two boys made an effort to trace the footprints to learn the direction the Hardys' enemies had taken, but lost them where the tracks connected with tyre marks.

"We'd never catch those men now, anyway," Frank said as they gave up. "Let's go back to the cave and see if we can find any clues."

He went on to say that if something large and heavy had been hidden inside, the cave might have other chambers, perhaps purposely blocked from view by piled-up rocks.

Callie and Iola, and even Chet, showed signs of their recent ordeal, so Frank and Joe decided to call off their sleuthing for that evening. The group piled into their cars and drove to the farm.

Mr and Mrs Morton hurried out on to the front porch as soon as they heard the cars arrive. "Thank goodness you're all safe!" Mrs Morton exclaimed, throwing her arms round her son and the two girls.

Chet and Iola's father said little, but smiled his relief, and gave Frank and Joe each a warm handshake "We're mighty grateful to you boys!" he murmured.

Mrs Morton served a hot dinner for everyone while Callie Shaw telephoned her parents. Later, as the whole group sat in the living-room, Iola exclaimed:

"Oh, I almost forgot! Look what I found this afternoon. It was on the ground just outside the cave."

Iola fetched her overall and reached into the pocket to take out a gold cuff link. In it was set a bluish fluorescent amber, cut in the shape of a tiger.

The Hardys stared at each other, then Joe cried out, "One of the cuff links Dad told us to try to find!"

· 8 ·

Stolen Evidence

ONLY the Hardy boys knew the significance of Iola's find. She asked innocently, "You mean your father lost this cuff link?"

"No, but it has something to do with a case he's working on," Frank revealed. "I'm afraid I can't tell you any more than that."

Iola had turned the cuff link over. "Here's some Oriental wording on the back," she said. "Let's ask Jim Foy to come out and decipher it."

Frank and Joe telephoned their friend at once. He said he would drive over. When the Chinese-American boy arrived, he gazed at the cuff link in amazement.

"These symbols are Cantonese and mean Hong Kong," he translated. "And this beautiful bluish amber is highly prized by the Chinese. It is often used for carving little figures of Buddha-sitting-in-the-lotus."

Jim went on to relate that amber was called "tiger soul" in old Chinese legends. It was believed that when a tiger died, its spirit penetrated the earth and turned to amber.

"I don't know whether there's a spirit in this," Chet spoke up, "but I do know it came from Hong Kong and so did the *Hai Hau*. I'll bet this cuff link was part of the smugglers' contraband on it!"

"You could be right," Frank said reflectively. "Well, one thing's sure. They won't be back to the cave. Whatever they had hidden in there they've taken away."

"One guess," said Joe. "Boxes of smuggled goods."

"I don't like this," Chet grumbled. "Sounds to me as if all of us are getting mixed up with a gang of smugglers!"

Frank and Joe themselves felt a little worried. They had been suspicious that members of the Chinese factions interested in the *Hai Hau* might trail them to Bayport. The cave incident would seem to prove they had. But how did the Chameleon fit into the picture of the smuggling racket?

"Did those men you heard at the cave sound like Chinese?" Frank asked Chet and the girls.

Iola and Callie debated this. Neither had noticed a foreign accent, they said.

Chet shrugged. "We couldn't tell for sure. We caught only a few words."

Frank asked Iola if he might take the cuff link with him. She agreed, and Joe slipped the piece of jewellery into an envelope she gave him and put it in his pocket.

When the excitement died down, Mr Morton picked up a copy of the evening newspaper and began turning the pages. Suddenly he remarked, "That's quite an advertisement you fellows dreamed up." He chuckled. "Almost makes *me* want to take a ride on your junk!"

"Let's see, Dad!" Iola exclaimed excitedly. She sprang up and went to perch on the arm of her father's armchair. Chet and Callie looked over her shoulder. The announcement read:

Have fun sailing to Rocky Isle aboard a fabulous Chinese

junk. It's the oldest in sailing, yet the newest in today's exciting boat age. Made to order for Bayport swash-bucklers. The exotic Hai Hau *brings an exciting glimpse of the mysterious Orient to Barmet Bay. The boating adventure of a lifetime. Three return trips a day!*

"Wow!" Chet said. "That ought to bring us business!" He beamed with anticipation.

"What do you mean us?" Joe winked at the others. "You'll probably be off spelunking somewhere."

"How did you guess?" Chet admitted, grinning. "I've made up my mind to explore the right-hand fork of that tunnel—if I can squeeze through, that is. But don't worry, fellows. I'll serve on the crew later."

When the gathering finally broke up, Frank and Joe took Callie Shaw home. Then they drove directly to their own home. The Hardy house lay dark and silent in the moonlight.

"Guess Aunt Gertrude's asleep," said Frank. "What say we test the cuff link for fingerprints?"

The boys went down to the basement, where Frank took out their kit of detective equipment. He dusted the jewellery for fingerprints, then examined the results under a magnifying glass.

"This has Iola's prints on it," Joe announced, after comparing them with an inked set on a card. The Hardys had built up a sizeable fingerprint file, including records on all their family and acquaintances. "If there were any other prints, Iola's have blurred them out."

"Let's phone Dad just the same," Frank proposed and put in the call to Los Angeles.

To the boys' disappointment, neither Mr nor Mrs

Hardy was in the hotel, so Frank requested that his parents call back early in the morning.

Joe yawned. "Let's go to bed, Frank."

The next morning at the breakfast table Joe asked his aunt what she had found out about Dr Montrose. "Do you still think he's in league with that broker pal of his to swindle people?"

In response Miss Hardy did a rare thing—she blushed! "I'm ashamed to tell you boys I didn't learn a thing. Instead, I went to sleep!"

"What!"

"Dr Montrose gave me a pill to take, then he kept talking about how I felt, so I couldn't get started on the other topic."

"Where was Mrs Witherspoon all this time?" Frank put in.

"Oh, wandering round the house. She's—uh—kind of an inquisitive person," Miss Hardy replied. "Pretty soon my head began to nod. I remember the doctor saying, 'Why don't you go upstairs and have a good sleep? We'll leave now, Mrs Witherspoon.' They left and I started upstairs. The next thing I knew I woke up in my room. The clock said ten minutes past twelve —I could scarcely believe my eyes!"

Frank told his aunt that Chet had come there and found the door open. "I guess it's my fault," she said, and berated herself for such carelessness. "An invitation to sneak thieves!" She hurried to check the silver in the dining-table drawer. It was intact.

"And of course the alarm didn't go off and alert you that Chet was approaching the house," Joe remarked.

"It certainly won't happen again," Miss Hardy

declared. "But you know I do feel better—in fact, I'm fine."

At that moment the telephone rang. Joe answered. "It's Dad!" he exclaimed. Frank hurried to join his brother in the front hall. "He's calling long distance from the West Coast," Joe added. Both boys shared the phone during the conversation that followed. They told their father eagerly about the *Hai Hau* and the exciting events following its purchase. Joe also mentioned the two visits by mysterious prowlers and finally the finding of the one cuff link.

"Amazing!" the detective exclaimed. "I probably should come home to pursue this cuff-link clue. On the other hand, it may tie in with a new lead I have—that the Chameleon has recently had some business with certain Chinese in California. I believe I'll stay here, since he may be in this vicinity."

Frank asked, "How's your case coming along, Dad?"

"Not much luck yet," Fenton Hardy reported. "I need certain data from my safe. Get out all the top-secret records on Balarat and shoot them to me here in Los Angeles by airmail special delivery. You'll find them in a Manila packet labelled *The Chameleon*."

"We'll send it right away, Dad."

"Fine! See you later, boys! Goodbye."

The brothers hurried upstairs to their father's study. Joe dialled the secret combination of the safe, then opened the safe door.

He stared inside, gulped, and cried out in dismay, "The file on the Chameleon is gone!"

Frank nodded, grim-lipped. "This'll be a blow to Dad. That envelope contained all his private evidence against the Chameleon." He grabbed his brother's arm. "Do you know what this means? One of the Chameleon's henchmen must be watching this house. When he saw the front door open, he walked in without the alarm going off."

"Right. And, Joe, he must be an expert at safe-cracking! I think we'd better notify Dad at once."

"First, let's see if anything else is missing," Joe suggested.

On the inside of the safe door the boys' father had pasted a printed list of the contents. As Joe read each item, Frank checked. Finally he said, "Everything's here. That burglar only wanted the Chameleon file."

Frank placed the call to his father's hotel in Los Angeles. Fenton Hardy took the bad news with little comment, but said he was disturbed for the safety of the boys and his sister.

"You'd better be extra careful from now on," the detective warned. "And call the police to investigate."

"Right, Dad!" Frank said.

Within five minutes after the young sleuth had phoned headquarters, a police car arrived at the house. Chief Collig hurried inside, accompanied by two plain-clothesmen, Hanley and Darkle.

"Now then, what happened?" Chief Collig demanded.

Frank gave the details of the robbery, then led the men upstairs to the study. Joe followed.

Collig and Hanley examined the safe. The latter dusted it for prints, but found none.

"Smart operator," he remarked. "Wiped off all traces clean as a whistle!"

Chief Collig nodded shrewdly. "He'd *have* to be smart

to open this job without blowing it." Turning back to the boys, the chief said, "I didn't have time to check my files on the Chameleon. What's the story on him?"

Frank explained that he was an international thief and confidence man, whose real name was Arnold Balarat. Originally from New York, Balarat had operated all over the United States and in Europe, as well as on ocean liners.

"The Trans-Ocean Lines engaged Dad to find him after he swindled a number of their passengers," Frank concluded. "The FBI is certain that Balarat is now in this country. Dad's been hunting for him out on the West Coast after some clues turned up in Los Angeles. But so far the Chameleon is still at large."

Together the police and the Hardy boys looked for clues to the identity of the burglar. They found none and Chief Collig shook his head, perplexed. "That man left no fingerprints. Well, we'll talk to the neighbours about seeing any prowlers and find out what they have to offer."

After the officers left, Frank said, "I suggest we phone Mrs Witherspoon and Dr Montrose. They may have seen someone."

He spoke to Mrs Witherspoon first. "Oh, how dreadful! A robbery!" she said . . . "No, Frank, I didn't see anyone. I hope you catch him soon. I'm too weak to talk any more. I'll have to see Dr Montrose. Goodbye."

Frank now phoned the doctor himself. His line was engaged. In a few minutes Frank tried again. Still engaged. After a third try he proposed that he and Joe stop at Dr Montrose's office on their way to the dock.

"Good enough," his brother agreed.

They said goodbye to Aunt Gertrude, then hurried off in their convertible. Frank parked at the front of Dr Montrose's office in the town centre. Entering, they found themselves in a comfortable waiting room. Apparently the doctor employed no receptionist.

"Hey, take a look at some of these," Joe murmured in a low voice.

He pointed to a number of framed letters hanging on the walls. They were glowing testimonials from former patients. An ornate diploma stated that Hubert Montrose had been awarded the degree of Doctor of Medicine from Ardvor College.

Frank grinned. "Mighty impressive!"

The brothers seated themselves in two of the leather chairs. Presently Dr Montrose came from a back room. A look of surprise flickered across his face, but this was quickly replaced by a smooth professional smile.

"Ah, good morning!" He shook hands with his two visitors. "Tell me, how is your aunt?"

"Much better, thanks," Frank said.

Dr Montrose did not invite the boys into his consulting room. He evidently had a patient inside. "Just what can I do for you?" he inquired.

Frank explained about the robbery and asked if the doctor had noticed anything unusual during his visit to the house.

Dr Montrose frowned thoughtfully. "Now that you mention it, I did hear a noise upstairs just as I was leaving," he replied. "However, I assumed it was a maid or one of the family moving about."

"That was the robber!" Frank cried.

"Oh, I'm sorry," said Dr Montrose. "But I'm afraid

I can't help any more. And now, if you'll excuse me—"

The Hardys left and started for the pier. A block from the waterfront they saw Biff Hooper coming from a shop, his arms loaded with crates of fruit drink. They stopped and he hopped into the car.

"Hey, what kept you guys?" Biff asked. "We have a full load of passengers."

"Swell!" Joe told him.

"Sure is," Frank added.

The Hardys found a gay crowd gathered on the pier to watch the *Hai Hau* leave. The passengers were already aboard.

"How about that?" said Tony proudly as he came up and showed Frank and Joe the cash receipts. "Full the first trip!"

Frank beamed, slapped his friend on the back, and climbed aboard. The *Hai Hau*'s owners took their places. Jim Foy cast off amid shouts and waves from the spectators. Biff revved the outboard and Frank steered out across Barmet Bay.

It was a fine sunny morning, promising a most enjoyable voyage to Rocky Isle. Joe and Tony hoisted the sails to take advantage of the slight breeze. The passengers called out in delight as the junk rode the waves.

Presently Frank noticed that the stern was riding low in the water. Setting the wheel, he went to open the afterdeck hatch, then gave a low cry of alarm. The shallow compartment below was filled with water!

"Hey, fellows! Come here!" When they arrived, he whispered hoarsely, "We've sprung a leak!"

The boys' faces filled with alarm. *Could they possibly make the island safely with their boatload of passengers?*

· 9 ·

Wharf Chase

"WE'RE letting in water too fast!" Joe said, peering into the compartment. "At this rate we'll capsize before we get to Rocky Isle!"

"What'll we do?" Biff gasped.

"We'd better come about and try to make it back to Bayport," Frank said. "I'll start the bilge pump!"

As the boys changed sail and turned the junk round, the passengers plied them with anxious questions. Consternation spread when they learned the *Hai Hau* was leaking.

"We should have known better than to trust ourselves in a crazy boat like this!" a stout woman stormed.

"You're right, dear," agreed her husband, a very thin man in a flowered sports shirt. "We should've listened to Clams Dagget when he said this junk was nothing *but* junk!"

Joe stifled the angry retort that rose to his lips, and Frank said, "Please be calm, everyone. We'll get you safely back to Bayport."

"You'd better!" the stout woman snapped.

Meanwhile, the action of the bilge pump had stemmed the flood of water pouring into the compartment. The source of the leak was now visible—a gaping hole several inches in diameter.

"Hey!" a man in the bow called out. "You mentioned Clams Dagget. Isn't that his boat over there?"

A motor launch was speeding towards them. "That's Clams, all right!" a high school youth confirmed.

The girl beside him clutched his arm happily. "Thank goodness!" She sighed. "Now we'll all be saved!"

The other passengers cheered.

The crew of the *Hai Hau* felt too disgusted and heartsick to comment. Joe and Tony had crawled down into the compartment below the afterdeck and were plugging the leak with socks and sweaters.

"That hole was no accident," Tony muttered between clenched teeth. "Look!" He picked up a round piece of wood floating on the water in the compartment.

"Look," Frank replied, disturbed. "Someone made it with a keyhole saw from the outside. After a while the wood gave way."

By the time the leak was stopped, Clams Dagget's motor launch, the *Sandpiper*, had arrived within hailing range of the *Hai Hau*. In response to shouts from the junk's passengers, he pulled alongside.

"What'sa matter, boys? Havin' trouble keepin' that Chinese bathtub afloat?" Clams taunted with a sneering grin. To the others aboard, he added, "Just climb over into my launch, folks. I'll get you to Rocky Isle safe and sound. I coulda told you that old hulk wasn't seaworthy!"

"You did tell them!" Tony said angrily. "Maybe you had something to do with this leak, too!"

"You tryin' to say I caused it?" Clams roared.

"I sure wouldn't be surprised!"

The rest of the exchange was drowned out by the passengers clamouring for their money back. The boys refunded all fares, then assisted the people to climb over into the motor launch.

As it sped away, the *Hai Hau*'s crew looked at one another in deep chagrin. Biff revved the outboard to top speed and they headed back to Bayport.

Reaching a repair dock, the junk was hoisted out of water and thoroughly examined. The boys spent the next few hours pounding in a plug, covering it with a steel plate, and caulking the patch securely. When they finished, the *Hai Hau* was as seaworthy as ever.

"Neat job," said Biff, wiping his hands on a rag. "But I'd sure like to know if Clams *did* saw that hole."

"We can't prove he's the guilty party," Frank reminded the others. "If those Chinese we tangled with in New York are here in Bayport, they might have done it."

Late that afternoon, after Frank and Joe had returned home, Jim Foy stopped at the house. He said he had brought a letter from his uncle in Chinatown. It contained information not only about George Ti-Ming, but Chin Gok as well, gleaned through the Chinese Benevolent Association.

"Better read it yourselves," Jim advised.

The report stated that Chin Gok and Ti-Ming were the New York agents for two rival Chinese export firms based in Hong Kong. Both firms had been in trouble with United States and British authorities on smuggling charges. During the past few years, however, Ti-

Ming's group seemed to have stayed within the law.

"Ti-Ming became a travelling salesman, so far as anyone knows, and is rarely in New York any more," Mr Foy concluded in his letter.

The Hardys thanked him, and Jim left. That evening, the brothers were discussing the report in their room when Joe jumped up impetuously.

"What's eating you?" Frank asked.

"Hunch. Plain hunch that someone may try tampering with the *Hai Hau* again. I'd feel better sleeping there tonight."

"You have a point," Frank agreed. "But what about the dock watchman?"

"He doesn't have eyes in the back of his head," Joe said cryptically.

"That's right," Frank agreed. "We'll tell Aunt Gertrude."

When the brothers relayed their idea to her, she nodded assent. "If you decide to come back here any time during the night, phone first, or call on the radio— I'll turn it on," she directed, "because if the burglar alarm goes off, I'll certainly call the police at once."

Frank and Joe kissed her goodnight and drove to the dock.

"Let's look up Mike the watchman and tell him our plan," Frank said.

They hunted around but could not find Mike. Frank, indicating a nearby warehouse, remarked, "Doesn't he guard that too? Maybe he's inside. Let's look."

They found the great sliding door to the pitch-black building half-open. Frank snapped on his light and entered, then stepped back in consternation.

Mike lay on the floor unconscious, bleeding from a deep gash in his head!

Frank leaned over and began counting the pulse beat in Mike's wrist. "Pretty feeble," he announced.

Seeing a wall telephone, Joe put in a call to police headquarters. Meanwhile, Frank was using thumb pressure to stop the bleeding. A few minutes later a police car and an ambulance arrived. Mike was lifted on to a stretcher and carried away as the two officers, Hanley and Darkle, began to question the Hardys.

Frank was busy giving them full details when Joe, who had gone outside, exclaimed suddenly, "Frank, I just spotted two guys sneaking round the cabin of the junk! Let's see what they're up to!"

As he spoke, the shadowy figures reappeared, scrambling to the dock.

"There they are!" Joe cried out.

His voice must have carried. With a glance in the boys' direction, the intruders raced off along the wharf. The Hardys and the two policemen sped after them. The fugitives darted past parked cars and piled-up freight crates, and disappeared into an old warehouse.

"We have 'em trapped!" Joe exulted.

"Maybe!" Frank muttered.

When the four pursuers reached the warehouse, Hanley tried a small door, which yielded to his push. A faint scuffle of footsteps reached the ears of the four as they entered.

"I'll use my pocket flash," Joe whispered.

Frank grabbed his arm. "No sense in making targets of ourselves."

Hanley was groping along the wall. Finding a light switch, he clicked it on. Dim illumination flared from bulbs on the rafters overhead. The warehouse was stacked with bales and crated goods.

"Now what?" Joe murmured.

"Stay behind Darkle and me," Hanley ordered, as the officers began a search among the piled-up merchandise.

The next moment a faint bang came from the farthest corner of the warehouse. The Hardys and the police converged towards the source of the sound.

"A trap door!" Frank exclaimed, pointing to the floor. "And no ring to pull it open."

Hanley pried it up and Joe pointed his flashlight down the hole. A slime-covered ladder led downwards to dark, oily water. Evidently this part of the warehouse jutted out on pilings. The next moment the group heard a splash of oars dwindling in the distance.

"What a break!" Joe groaned. "Those men must have had a rowing-boat hidden under here!"

The boys rushed out of the warehouse with the police and down to the waterfront. They peered out, straining their eyes for a glimpse of the rowing-boat, but it had disappeared.

"We've lost 'em!" Frank muttered. "And I'll bet they're the ones who slugged Mike."

"I'll ask the harbour patrol to look for them," Hanley said.

"In the meantime, Joe and I will go aboard the *Hai Hau* and see what those fellows were up to."

A fresh shock awaited the Hardys when they went aboard. The cabin was in wild disorder, with bunk cushions pulled out and accessories strewn about the deck.

"Those men must have been searching for something!" Frank said worriedly.

A brief check indicated that no serious damage had been done to the junk and nothing was missing. Relieved but baffled, the boys restored order, all the while speculating on what the intruders had been looking for.

"Probably contraband," Frank guessed. "Wonder if they found any."

"I doubt it," said Joe. "Every place they tore up we'd already examined."

Hanley and Darkle came aboard. They too were puzzled by the mysterious search.

"You fellows may as well go home," Hanley told them. "The police will look after your junk from now on."

"Swell," said Frank.

He and Joe went to their car and at once turned on the short-wave radio. In a moment they were talking to Aunt Gertrude.

When she heard that they planned to return home, she remarked, "Good! You'll be much safer in your own beds! I'll watch out the window for you."

As soon as they reached the house, the brothers used the upstairs extension to call first one, then another, of the co-owners of the *Hai Hau* to tell them what had happened. Tony was angry, Biff annoyed, Chet a little scared.

Only Jim Foy seemed genuinely alarmed. "I do not like this," he said. "The junk must be most carefully guarded. Some evil influence is at work."

"I sure agree," said Joe, who was talking to him. "Well, see you in the morning."

The Chinese boy had just said goodbye when the alarm buzzer sounded throughout the house.

"Oh—oh!" Joe exclaimed. "The prowler again?" He and Frank dashed downstairs to nab him. When the doorbell rang almost instantly, the boys relaxed. Evidently the caller was friendly.

Aunt Gertrude was already answering the ring. She gasped as a huge Chinese towered in the doorway.

"Chin Gok!" Frank murmured, as he and Joe came down the steps.

"Well, what is it you want?" Miss Hardy demanded, a trifle shakily.

The Chinese man bowed low. "I wish to speak to the young men," he answered.

"Aunt Gertrude, this is Mr Chin Gok," Frank spoke up. Miss Hardy nodded.

"I would not trouble you at this time, but it is a matter of the utmost importance," Chin Gok went on. His voice was polite but insistent.

"All right. Step inside." Frank held the door open and Chin Gok entered, ducking his melon-shaped head. The Hardys ushered him into the living-room and they all sat down.

"What have you come to see us about?" Joe opened the conversation.

"About the junk which you purchased in New York. Once again I beg you most earnestly to sell it to my humble self. Name your own price!"

The boys glanced at each other but remained silent.

Chin Gok went on, "I will admit to you certain interests in Hong Kong are most anxious to obtain the *Hai Hau.*"

"What interests?" Frank challenged.

"A group of religious worshippers," the huge Chinese replied. "You see, the *Hai Hau* is a sacred boat to my people. Once it was used to transport a large statue of Buddha from Singapore to Hong Kong. I repeat—we will pay any price you ask, within reason!"

The Hardys were more mystified than ever. Also, they were tempted by the chance to realize a large profit. In view of all the difficulties they were having, it might be wiser to sell the junk. On the other hand, Frank and Joe hated the thought of giving up an unsolved mystery, and besides, they would have no summer job.

Just then the telephone rang and Frank went to the instrument in the hall. A moment later he gasped. Putting down the phone, he beckoned Joe to join him.

"Wow! Wait till you hear this!" he whispered.

· 10 ·

Shore Pirates!

"WHAT's up?" Joe asked his brother excitedly.

Frank shot a quick glance towards the living-room from which Chin Gok was watching the boys with intense curiosity, then replied in a low voice:

"That was a telegram from Ti-Ming. It said, 'Don't sell the *Hai Hau* at any price or the curse it carries will descend on you!'"

Joe was startled, but was careful to show no outward sign of this, since Chin Gok's eyes were still fastened on the Hardys.

"Looks as if Ti-Ming's trying to throw a scare into us," Joe murmured.

"Could be," Frank replied. "But why? Anyway, let's not give Chin Gok any encouragement about buying the *Hai Hau*."

"Agreed."

The brothers rejoined Aunt Gertrude and the Chinese caller. Frank addressed Chin Gok. "We'll think over your offer, but we don't plan to sell."

Chin Gok dropped his air of exaggerated politeness. A look of rage twisted his features. Losing his temper completely, he stood up and shrilled, "You—you fools—" and burst into a torrent of Chinese.

Aunt Gertrude drew herself up. "You cannot talk to my nephews that way!" she said icily. "You will leave immediately." She gestured towards the front door.

Chin Gok, although still muttering angrily, retreated slowly. The instant he was on the front porch, Miss Hardy shut the door firmly.

Joe looked at his aunt admiringly. "Wow! You really convinced him you meant business!"

Aunt Gertrude frowned. "Yes. But I almost wish you boys had sold him that junk. I have a feeling it will only bring more trouble."

Frank spoke up. "Joe and I can't give up work on this mystery now." Joe nodded vigorously.

The next morning the Hardys and their partners assembled at the Chinese junk. Although only four passengers bought tickets for the trip to Rocky Isle, the boys refused to let their spirits be dampened.

"Heave ho!" Tony sang out as he cast off.

Several people on the dock made sarcastic comments as the *Hai Hau* pulled away from the pier.

"You got plenty of life rafts aboard?" called one man derisively.

"Don't need 'em," Biff called back, unruffled. "We just had a swell repair job on the hull."

His confident manner and words allayed any qualms the junk's passengers might have had. Everyone relaxed, and soon were laughing and singing as the *Hai Hau* glided across the bay.

Once on Rocky Isle, the four travellers enjoyed a refreshing swim and leisurely picnic. The boys returned for a second group. This time there were five.

When the *Hai Hau* returned to its pier on the last trip

back, the owners felt that it had been a most successful day, even though there had not been a capacity number of passengers on either excursion.

"Simply thrilling!" a pleasant-faced woman exclaimed as she disembarked. "I've always wanted to sail in one of these Chinese ships and I enjoyed every minute of it!"

The other passengers added their delighted comments, which could be clearly heard by the group of spectators on the dock.

"We're over the hump!" Tony chuckled, and his companions grinned happily.

After the onlookers had dispersed, Frank said to his partners, "What say we give the junk another going-over tonight and hunt for hidden smugglers' loot?"

"You don't have to ask me twice," Tony answered.

"Same here," the others spoke up.

Biff added, "But let's not make our search at the dock."

The boys arranged to meet after supper and sail to some secluded spot up the bay where they could conduct their investigation undetected.

When the Hardy group, including Chet, gathered on the pier at the appointed time, Biff remarked wryly, "Boy, we sure could have picked a better evening!"

Tony glanced at the overcast sky. "You said it! We'd better keep a weather eye out for a storm."

The humidity had risen steadily since late afternoon, making the air hot and muggy. Not a breath of wind stirred.

Frank started the outboard and they set off. As the

Hai Hau pulled away from the pier, lightning flecked the horizon.

"Oh—oh! Hope that's just heat lightning," Chet muttered.

The boys cruised offshore and finally picked a hidden cove several miles from Bayport to drop anchor. The Shore Road ran close to the beach at this point, but a row of large willows partially screened the junk from anyone using the road.

For over an hour the Hardys and their chums searched the *Hai Hau* from stem to stern. But no hidden cache was revealed. By now the stormy-looking sky had become very dark.

Frank lit a pair of lanterns, quipping, "Okay, team. Night shift coming up."

Chet wiped his perspiring forehead. "Say, boss, don't we get time out for a snack? I'm hungry."

The plump youth's eyes had fallen on a bag of biscuits which Jim Foy had brought along. Jim chuckled and passed the bag around. "Thought these would come in handy."

Biff bit into one of the crisp cookies. The next moment he said, "Hey! What's this little paper inside?"

"Pull it out and learn your future." Jim grinned. "These are Chinese fortune cookies."

Biff extracted the tiny strip of paper. He read aloud: "GREAT WEALTH IS IN STORE!"

"We'd better keep looking for that smugglers' loot!" Biff exclaimed in glee. "Maybe it's pirate gold!"

Laughing, the other boys examined their own fortunes. Frank's warned, "YOUR BEAUTIFUL EYES SPELL TROUBLE," and the others roared with laughter. Joe's advised him not to trust a certain red-haired girl he would meet.

"Good advice," Biff remarked. "Iola wouldn't like her, anyway."

Tony's fortune told of an impending discussion with a stocky, dark man. "My dad probably," Tony joked. "He'll have a few things to say if I get home late!"

Chet was looking indignantly at his paper. "Huh! Mine says, BEWARE! YOU EAT TOO MUCH!"

His friends burst out laughing. "Better not finish that biscuit," Frank said with mock gravity.

"You guys don't understand," the stout boy asserted. "I just need lots of nourishment for all the work I do!"

His words were greeted with fresh merriment. "Listen! I'll bet you're too out of condition to balance on the rail of this junk!" Joe dared him.

"Is that so? Just watch!" Chet boasted.

Before anyone could advise caution, the chunky lad climbed up on the gunwale. He swayed precariously, arms outstretched. The next moment Chet gave a wild yell and toppled overboard. Feet first, he hit the water with a mighty splash and disappeared beneath the surface. His friends held their sides and quaked with merriment.

"For Pete's sake!" Joe said. "I didn't think he'd really try that stunt."

Chet bobbed to the surface. Sputtering, he pulled himself up, grabbed the *Hai Hau*'s bowline, then to his comrades' complete astonishment, swam rapidly to shore. Dashing up on to the beach, Chet hitched the line around a gnarled old tree stump.

"Okay, this'll show you guys!" he shouted. "If you

want to get back to Bayport, you'll either have to untie this end of the rope or leave it behind."

"That rope's valuable," Frank commented, and added, grinning, "Looks as if the joke's on us!" Joe started to remove his shirt and slacks in order to swim ashore. Just then a car's headlight beams swept off the road and blazed between the trees. It was a jeep which plunged across the sandy beach. A moment later it ground to a halt and four masked men leaped out!

"Hey, what's going on?" Tony exclaimed, utterly astounded.

The crew of the *Hai Hau* stared dumbfounded for a moment as the men raced towards Chet.

"They must be after the junk!" Frank gasped. "If they're armed—look out! Chet!" he shouted. "Run!"

The stout boy did not run away, but he suddenly spun into action and untied the bowline.

"Don't wait for me!" he yelled, and hurled the line out into the water.

As the four assailants closed in on Chet, Joe declared he was going to jump overboard and help Chet.

Biff deterred him. "Those men are after the boat. If they don't get it, they'll let Chet go."

Although the Hardys were sceptical, they listened to their friend's advice. Frank immediately began issuing orders.

"We'll leave, then sneak back and pick up Chet."

While the other boys hauled in the anchor and the dripping bowline, he gunned the outboard into life. Two of the masked men plunged into the water and swam swiftly towards the junk. But the *Hai Hau* was already backing speedily out of the cove, beyond their reach. An unintelligible snarl echoed across the water, and the two swimmers returned to shore.

"Put out the lanterns!" Frank directed Tony.

Once clear of the cove, he rounded a spit of land, stopped the engine, and let the junk drift through the darkness towards a concealing clump of trees and shrubbery.

"Now what?" Jim Foy asked in a whisper.

"You stay aboard and guard the junk!" said Frank, grabbing a waterproof flashlight. "The rest of us will go over the side and rescue Chet!"

Swiftly but silently the Hardys, Biff, and Tony lowered themselves into the water. A few quick strokes brought them to shore. Then they plunged through the trees like darting shadows, hoping to circle round and take the masked assailants from the rear, if they were still there.

As the boys emerged in sight of the beach, they saw the four men dragging Chet, still kicking and squirming, towards their car.

"They're kidnapping him to hold as a hostage!" Joe exclaimed.

"Make plenty of noise," Frank whispered to his companions. Out loud he shouted, "*Take 'em, gang!*"

Yelling like Indians on the warpath, the boys burst from cover. Chet's captors whirled round. The stout lad seized his chance, pulled himself free, and unleashed a flurry of blows.

A second later Frank, Joe, Biff and Tony waded in, fists swinging! A brief but wild melée followed. Confused and taken off guard, the masked men turned and fled towards the jeep.

Biff made a flying tackle and grabbed one by the ankle, but the fellow kicked himself free and went tearing after his companions.

"Stop 'em!" Joe yelled as the jeep's engine roared.

At that moment a vivid bolt of lightning flashed across the cove. Simultaneously a deafening *crack* split the air. The boys halted in their chase as a single thought struck their minds.

Had the Hai Hau been struck by lightning?

· 11 ·

A Peculiar Theft

"COME on!" Frank urged the others. "Let's check on the *Hai Hau*!"

The boys darted back across the beach. They were about to take a short cut through the grove of trees when Frank suddenly halted. He grabbed Joe's arm and pointed to the water's edge.

"Look! That's what was hit!"

By his flashlight he showed the others where a tree had been split apart by the bolt of lightning.

Tony shuddered. "Whew! If the lightning had hit just the other side of the cove—no more *Hai Hau*!"

Relieved, the five companions made their way across the narrow spit of land enclosing the cove. When they emerged through the cluster of trees and brush, they saw the junk lying safely offshore.

"Oh, you beauteous doll!" Tony gave a mimicking hugging gesture.

Jim Foy hailed the boys as they swam back and climbed aboard. "Nice going, fellows! You were a real hero, Chet!" he added, slapping the stout youth on the back.

"He sure was," Frank agreed. "Untying that line gave us a chance to save the *Hai Hau*."

THE MYSTERY OF THE CHINESE JUNK   93

"Shucks, it was nothing," Chet said, beaming modestly but enjoying the praise. "Any of you fellows would have done the same."

"Except that we wouldn't have tied the junk up in the first place." Biff grinned.

Frank asked seriously, "How do you suppose those men knew where we had taken the *Hai Hau*?"

No one ventured an answer but Joe. "They may be part of a gang and have spies dotted here and there along the shore to help them."

Chet whistled. "You mean smugglers?"

"Could be. Or boat thieves."

Tony spoke up. "Fellows, let's get back to Bayport and then talk this over. The sky's going to fall in any second."

Frank started the engine. A stiff breeze had sprung up suddenly and to increase speed Biff and Tony hoisted sail.

"Wow! We're in for a real blow, mates!" Joe cried, as the junk raced before the wind.

The boys shivered in their wet clothes. Suddenly a jagged streak of lightning illumined the heavens. It was followed by a crashing boom of thunder. A second later the rain poured down in gusty sheets.

A heavy swell was running. As the waves increased in height, Frank shouted, "Douse the sail!"

The crew hastened to comply. Soon the junk was rolling and pitching wildly amid mountainous breakers. One moment the bow would shoot up as the craft raced towards the crest of a wave; the next moment it would plunge into the trough with the stern lifted and the propeller racing out of water.

"O-o-oh! I—I feel sick!" Chet groaned, bracing himself against the cabin.

"Don't think about it. Help us get this centreboard down!" Tony commanded.

Frank clung to the tiller while the other boys made their way forward. The centre-board had swelled and jammed. Biff tried to force it clear with a boat hook.

Suddenly a wave smacked the junk on her port quarter. The boat yawed and started to broach too! A second later the *Hai Hau* was heeling far over in the trough as water poured across the deck.

Just in time the centre-board dropped. Tony immediately plunged to Frank's assistance. Between them, they righted the tiller and brought the junk back on course.

"Thanks, pal!" Frank gasped, blinking the water out of his eyes.

The boys were drenched to the skin. They huddled in the stern, hearts pounding, as the junk ploughed forward through the storm. When the lights of Bayport came into view, the weary sailors gave a grateful shout.

"Home, sweet home!" Biff exclaimed.

The storm had slackened considerably, and the *Hai Hau* was moored at the pier without difficulty.

"Boy, what a night!" Chet heaved a sigh as he climbed on to the pier. "We didn't find any pirate gold —but we sure found plenty of trouble!"

"How about you fellows coming up to the house and drying off?" Frank suggested. "You can call your folks from there."

"Let's do it," Chet urged the others and they agreed.

Fortunately, Frank had raised the top of the brothers'

convertible after parking, so the interior was dry. Biff and Tony got in. Jim Foy said he would ride with Chet in his jalopy.

Aunt Gertrude greeted the sodden group at the door. "Gracious!" she gasped. "Where *have* you boys been? You didn't go sailing in that junk on a night like this?"

"I'm afraid we did," Joe confessed.

Without waiting for further explanation, Miss Hardy said, "Go upstairs and put on dry clothes. Frank and Joe have enough extra for all of you," Aunt Gertrude added, although she eyed Chet's stout form askance. "I'll make some hot cocoa right away."

Later, after cups of steaming hot chocolate and chicken sandwiches, the boys felt revived. The four visitors had called their homes, and Aunt Gertrude had heard the story of the evening's adventures.

"Masked kidnappers!" she gasped. "Oh, what next. Did you call the police?"

Frank sprang up. "Good grief! I forgot all about it! Should've done that first thing. My brain must be waterlogged."

Chief Collig was astounded at Frank's report, and said he would put men immediately on the assailants' trail. "It looks as if they might be henchmen of one of those Chinese who's determined to get the *Hai Hau*," he stated.

Frank returned to his friends and relayed this idea. "Jim, how about keeping your eyes open for any Oriental strangers in town?"

"I'll do that," the Chinese-American agreed.

"But those men tonight didn't have Oriental accents," Chet spoke up. He suddenly snapped his fingers. "Say, they sounded like the guys that Callie and Iola and I heard talking in the cave," Chet declared.

Tony groaned. "This gets more complicated all the time! I sure hope you Hardys can work it all out. I can't!"

Before the boys said goodnight, they made plans for the following day. It was decided that Tony, Biff and Jim would sail the *Hai Hau* to Rocky Isle. The Hardys would join Chet in exploring the right-hand fork of the cave tunnel.

"They may even have left other clues in the cave that will help us crack this whole mystery!"

The next morning the sky was clear and the sun shone brightly. Frank and Joe had offered to pick up Chet at the Morton farm. They found their chum fully equipped with his spelunking gear, in spite of the summer heat. Joe teased him about it as they headed out the West Road.

"Never mind," Chet retorted. "This stuff may come in handy if we get in any tight spots."

"Tight spots are just what I'm worried about," Joe said with a grin. "We'll probably need a shoe-horn to pry you out in that getup!"

Frank pulled the convertible off the unpaved road, and the boys climbed the hillside to the cave. Entering, they made their way to the fork in the tunnel.

"A tight squeeze, all right," Frank muttered, noting the tiny entrance. "Well, here goes!"

Dropping to his hands and knees, he squirmed into the opening.

"You next." Joe grinned wryly at Chet. "I'll go last,

so I can pull you out by the feet if you get stuck!"

One by one, the boys wriggled through the cramped, pitch-black passageway. The trio emerged finally into a sizeable cavern. Here the glow of their flashlights and the illumination from Chet's helmet lamp enabled them to take in the whole chamber. From its roof hung stalactites, giving a fairyland appearance to the setting.

Suddenly Joe gave a cry. "Look! Someone's been here recently."

His eye had fallen on something lying on the floor of the cave. He snatched it up—a partially burned white envelope. Evidently the dampness had put out the flames.

"Frank!" Joe exclaimed, straightening the envelope and staring at it. "It's one from our house with a return name and address!"

His brother took one glance, and said tensely, "It must be the envelope you put the two hundred dollars in!"

"You mean this is that thief's hide-out?" Chet asked nervously. "Maybe he's one of the smugglers?"

Frank and Joe did not reply. Instead, they began a frantic search, thinking the two one-hundred-dollar bills might be hidden away in the cave. They did not find them, but under a fallen stalactite Chet pounced on another scrap of paper.

"Hey! Here's something else, fellows!"

It was part of a half-burned letter typed on business stationery. The torn-off fragment bore the following lines:

would advise you to get in on the ground floor while the

stock shares can still be purchased cheaply. The mining deposit is a rich one and the company is bound to realize tremendous profits during the next few

"I'll bet that thief uses his stolen money to buy stock," Chet guessed.

"Could be," Frank commented. "Chet, this is a real find. It could be our best clue so far to that burglar."

Joe mused aloud, "Typewriters all have distinguishing characteristics. If we can trace the machine this was written on, it may give us a real lead!"

"Do you think the burglar is part of some gang interested in the *Hai Hau*?" Chet asked.

"I wonder," Frank replied. "If so, they know this cave well. The sooner we get busy on this stock-letter clue the better. Let's go."

"Let's talk to Sam Radley about the case if he's back," Frank suggested as he started the convertible. "He's an expert on typewriter clues."

Sam Radley was Fenton Hardy's best detective. He had gone to Chicago recently to collect evidence needed in another case which Mr Hardy was handling.

"Fine idea," Joe agreed.

Frank dropped Chet off at the farm, then drove home. He telephoned Radley and learned that the detective had flown in to Bayport late the previous day. He promised to come over to the Hardy house at four o'clock that afternoon.

In the meantime, the brothers made fingerprint tests on the two pieces of paper. Only their own prints were revealed!

"That burglar is a slick customer," Joe remarked. "He must wear plastic gloves!"

"It's not hard for me to believe that he's also the safecracker," said Frank thoughtfully.

When Sam Radley arrived, the boys briefed the wiry, sandy-haired detective on developments in their mystery to date. Then Frank showed him the torn scrap of letter.

"You're a typewriter expert, Sam. Can you tell us what kind of machine this was written on?"

The detective studied the typewritten characters with a practised eye, then nodded. "This was done on a German-make machine, called the Zeus. Should be easy to trace. This particular style of type was used only on the first model which was imported to this country three years ago."

Radley asked to use the hall telephone and placed a call to the New York distributors for the Zeus typewriter. Within minutes he had the information he sought.

"They're sold locally through the Bayport Office Supply," Sam reported to the Hardys.

"Okay, let's go and talk to them," Joe said.

Radley drove the boys to the Bayport Office Supply Company in the town centre. In answer to their questions, the proprietor consulted his records and informed them that he had sold only four typewriters of that make and model.

"The Zeus is a fine machine," he said, "but it wasn't well known at that time—three years ago. I sold the four all in one batch to the Regent Hotel."

After thanking him, Radley and the two boys went to the hotel. Frank explained to the manager, Mr Irwin, that they were working on a case and would like to see the four Zeus typewriters which the hotel had purchased three years before.

"Certainly," Mr Irwin agreed. The manager led the three sleuths into the hotel's business office. Several women clerks were at work, typing or running accounting machines.

Radley, Frank and Joe examined samples of typing from each of the three Zeus typewriters in the office, and compared them with the letter.

"The 's' and the 'l' are both out of line in the letter and the tail of the 'e' is worn away," Sam observed. "None of these samples matches."

Frank turned to the manager. "We were told at the Bayport Office Supply Company that you bought *four* Zeuz typewriters. May we see the other one?"

"We had that one assigned for the use of our guests," Irwin replied. "But I'm afraid you're out of luck so far as checking it goes."

"Why?" Joe asked.

"The typewriter," Mr Irwin explained, "was stolen a month ago."

"Stolen!" the Hardys chorused.

The identical thought raced through the brothers' minds. Was the typewriter thief the same person who had stolen their two hundred dollars, Mr Hardy's file on the Chameleon, and perhaps owned the cuff link Iola had found?

· 12 ·

The Vanishing Visitor

FRANK suddenly snapped his fingers. "Maybe the type-writer was stolen by someone staying here," he said to the hotel manager. "May we look at the register?"

"Of course."

Mr Irwin led the Hardys and Sam Radley down-stairs to the foyer and requested the receptionist at the desk to show them the registration book. Frank and Joe flipped back the pages and began checking the names of guests who had registered at the hotel a month before.

"Oh—oh!"

Joe gave a surprised gasp and pointed to a signature written with a flourish—*Dr Hubert E Montrose*. Frank was equally intrigued.

"Find something?" the manager asked.

"An acquaintance of ours," Frank replied cautiously. "We didn't know he'd ever lived at this hotel."

"Let me see." Mr Irwin glanced at the register. "Oh, yes. Dr Montrose stayed here for a week or so when he first arrived in town." He looked at the broth-ers curiously, but they did not voice their suspicions.

Frank, instead, added nonchalantly, "Dr Montrose found a house here in Bayport?"

Mr Irwin nodded. "Yes, he's renting the old Varney mansion out on the Shore Road. Quite a show place in its day, but now it's rather run-down."

The sleuths thanked the manager for his co-operation and left. As soon as the three were seated in the car, Sam asked, "Who's this fellow Montrose?"

"A doctor who just started practising here in town," Frank explained. "Most of his patients seem to be elderly widows. Dr Montrose advises them on financial as well as medical matters, and refers them to a friend of his who deals in stocks."

The detective grinned as Joe told how Aunt Gertrude had vowed to prove the doctor a swindler but had gone to sleep instead.

Sam pulled away from the kerb and started for the Hardy house.

"This stock business is why I was interested in finding out where Dr Montrose lives," Joe went on. "It's just possible he can help us to locate the person who wrote the stock-selling letter and even stole our money!"

"I see," said Sam. "And that man in turn might point out the thief."

"Exactly. Let's call on the doctor at his house after dinner."

Sam Radley said he would not be able to go, but Frank and Joe decided to make the call, anyway. Sam had supper with Aunt Gertrude and the boys. Later, as the detective was leaving, Tony Prito stopped at the Hardys' to report on the day's boat trip to Rocky Isle. He told Frank and Joe that the *Hai Hau* had carried six passengers on each return trip. It had been an enjoyable excursion, with smooth sailing both ways.

"Swell," Frank commented. "Joe and I were just going out to do a little sleuthing. Want to come along?"

"Sure. What's up?" After hearing the plan, he said, "Let's go!"

The three boys piled into the Hardy's convertible. Frank drove through the outskirts of town, then took the Shore Road. Their headlights blazed through the gathering dust.

By the time they reached the old Varney mansion it was nearly dark. The house stood on a wooded promontory overlooking Barmet Bay. Frank slowed the car as they neared their destination and stopped at the entrance to the grounds. A heavy chain barred the way.

"We'll have to go on foot," he murmured.

The boys found a footpath, which wound amid trees and underbrush, fully screening their approach. On the boys' right, the hillside sloped down steeply towards a sandy beach.

Presently they came in sight of the mansion. Built many years before, the house was designed in ornate Victorian style with gabled roof and outjutting turrets. It was surrounded by large hemlock and cypress trees.

"Sort of a spooky-looking place," Joe remarked.

"You said it!" Tony agreed.

As if to confirm their words, an owl hooted mournfully from the trees.

"I think he heard you," Frank joked.

Most of the mansion's windows were hung with dilapidated shutters, but a single light gleamed through an unshuttered window on the ground floor. Frank suggested that they knock on the back door which was nearest. Apparently this part of the grounds had once been a formal garden, but it was now clogged with waist-high weeds and undergrowth.

"Take it easy," Frank advised.

But Joe, impetuous as usual, pressed forward without watching his step. Tripping on a vine, he went sprawling. He gave a slight groan.

"Hey! Hurt yourself?" Tony asked.

"Wrenched my shoulder a bit, I guess. Gave me a twinge—it'll ease up, though."

Joe got to his feet, and followed the others, this time with caution. A moment later all three froze as a figure ahead loomed out of the shadows at one side of the house. Apparently he had come from the front, which faced the bay.

Tall and stooped, the figure glided away from the mansion, losing itself among the trees and shrubbery on the hillside. His rather furtive manner instantly aroused the boys' suspicions.

"Let's go and see what he's doing," Joe urged.

Tony asked if the doctor lived alone.

"He's supposed to, according to what Mrs Witherspoon told Aunt Gertrude," Joe confided. "She says he has no relatives and no housekeeper."

"Maybe that man's a patient," Frank offered.

"Or a guard," Tony added.

Joe was unconvinced. "If he is, he won't mind talking to us. But if he's a burglar, Dr Montrose would thank us for nabbing him."

"You win," said Tony.

The trio moved forward quickly. Reaching the edge of the promontory, they could make out their quarry picking his way down the slope towards the bay.

"Easy does it, Joe," Frank warned, as his brother ploughed ahead.

Fortunately, the hillside was covered with tall grass and scrub, which afforded good footing. The boys managed to descend without turning their ankles or falling. As they reached the bottom, they could see the stooped man hurrying across the beach.

"We'd better speed up or we'll lose him," Joe exclaimed, as the man went up a hillock of rock and sand.

He looked back for a moment, then darted down the opposite side and was lost to view.

"He may leave in a boat," Joe remarked worriedly.

The boys sprinted forward. But by the time they reached the top of the hillock, the man was nowhere in sight.

"He's disappeared!" Tony groaned. "But where?"

"No! There he is!" Joe exclaimed, pointing off to the right.

A stooped figure had appeared near the water's edge, some yards away. Turning, he started back up the hillside towards the Shore Road.

"Hey! Wait a minute!" Joe yelled, and the boys ran after him. Surprisingly, the man made no effort to flee.

"Well, what is it?" he demanded in a familiar harsh, cracked voice.

"Clams Dagget!" Joe gasped as the boys caught up with him.

"You pests botherin' me again?" Clams showed no signs of discomposure at being detected. "Well, what do you want now?"

"We'd like to know why you were prowling around Dr Montrose's house," Frank said forthrightly.

Clams snorted. "You're crazy! Haven't been near that old mansion. Been here on the beach all evenin'!"

·13·

A Cryptic Threat

"DON'T give us that story!" Tony Prito said hotly to Clams Dagget. "We followed you all the way down the hill!"

The beachcomber flew into a rage. "Oh, you did, did you? Well, let me tell you young scamps a thing or two!"

In salty language, he informed the boys that they were wrong. Besides, they had no business poking their noses into his affairs. If he ever caught them trying to shadow him, he would have the law on them so fast it would make their heads spin.

"And while I'm at it, I'm going to give you Hardys some advice," Clams ranted. "From now on, you'd better stay away from Rocky Isle! That place is dangerous!"

"What's dangerous about it?" said Joe, a note of doubt in his voice.

Clams' eyes narrowed. "Some mighty queer things have been goin' on there. I've seen lights blinkin' at night, and they weren't bein' flashed by the park guard on the island. He'd 'a' been in bed, and nobody else is supposed to be on Rocky Isle after nine o'clock. It stands to reason, anybody tryin' to snoop—" Clams paused significantly, "might find that place real unhealthy night or day!"

Somewhat surprised by Clams' revelation, the young sleuths tried to elicit further information from him. But the elderly pilot only muttered, "Told you all I know— don't say I didn't warn you." He strode off in the dusk.

The boys trudged back up the hill and again approached the mansion. They rapped on first the front door, then the back. There was no answer.

"I guess the doctor's out," Frank said resignedly.

During the drive home, Frank remained thoughtful, mulling the evening's events over in his mind. Who was the tall, stooped man the boys had followed from Dr Montrose's house? And, if the old beachcomber's claims were true, could the mysterious lights be connected with the junk and the cave hide-out on the hillside?

The next morning when the Hardys arrived at the pier, they found their shipmates already on board the *Hai Hau*, preparing for the day's voyage. Tony was tuning up the outboard, while Biff and Jim were busy polishing woodwork. Chet was talking to prospective passengers.

"Hi, slowcoaches!" the chunky lad greeted the Hardys. "You fellows just get out of bed?"

The Hardys laughed and climbed aboard. Tony looked up from the engine and wiped an oil smear off his cheek. "Hey, Biff!" he called. "See if you can find my feeler gauges so I can check these breaker points. I think I left 'em in the cabin."

"Okay."

Biff disappeared into the junk's cabin. A moment

later he reappeared, then the boys heard a cry of amazement. Frank saw Biff reach down and pick up a piece of paper.

"Hey, look at this! Another threat!"

Frank, Joe and the others gathered round tensely to examine his find. The note was badly typed on cheap pad paper, with two words misspelled. It said:

> *Keep youre nose out of my*
> *busines or else!*

"Where'd you find this, Biff?" asked Tony, who had not seen him pick it up.

"It was lying on the deck wrapped round a stone. Someone must have thrown it up here last night!"

"Clams Dagget probably!" Tony growled. "This sounds just like him!"

"You may be right," Frank said. "We'd better compare this with the mining-stock letter and see how the typing checks out."

After a hurried conference, the Hardys decided to take the note back to their crime laboratory for immediate study. The other four boys would man the *Hai Hau* on its daily cruise to Rocky Isle.

Frank and Joe sped home. While Frank set up the magnifying camera and lights in their basement laboratory, Joe telephoned Sam Radley to report the latest find. The detective promised to come over at once and assist in analyzing the typed specimens.

When he arrived ten minutes later, Radley asked, "Found out yet who sent the threat?"

"We've just started photographing it," Joe reported. "We think they were both written on the same typewriter."

The detective examined the threatening note for a few moments. "Offhand, I'd say you're right. The three key letters check out at first glance, but we'll need precise measurements to prove it."

With Radley's help, the boys made a number of magnified close-ups of the typing. Then Frank took the films into the darkroom which the Hardys had rigged in one corner of the basement.

While he was busy with the developing, the radio crackled.

"*Hai Hau* calling Hardys!" Chet's voice came over the loud-speaker.

Joe hastily flicked on the transmitter. "Hardys to *Hai Hau*! Come in, please! . . . What's up?" he added.

"We just left the pier!" Chet reported excitedly. "And guess who's on board?"

"Skip the games!" Joe said. "Who?"

"Ti-Ming! He's one of our passengers!"

Joe was startled. Had the Chinese decided to make their next move out in the open? And if so, did this forebode trouble aboard the junk?

"Does he know you're calling?" Joe asked.

"I doubt it," Chet replied. "He's up in the bow, acting like a sightseer."

"Okay. Keep a watch on him. And remember, we have the safety of the passengers to think about—so don't let him pull any fast ones!"

"Roger!" the plump lad's voice acknowledged. "Over and out."

Frank and Joe worked closely with Sam Radley in analysing and comparing the threatening note and the mining-stock letter. Microscopic details and measurements proved that the typed characters were identical in both.

"No doubt about it. These were written on the same machine," Radley concluded. "However, they must have been typed by different people, judging from the way the keys were struck—not to mention these two misspelled words."

"That might've been intentional to throw us off the track," Frank pointed out.

The investigator nodded. "Could be. But it's not easy for a typist to disguise his touch."

"Maybe Tony was right about Clams writing the threatening note," Joe put in, "although I doubt that he's the one who stole the typewriter from the hotel."

"But it means he knows the thief," Frank speculated.

"Not necessarily," Radley said. "The machine could have been sold to an innocent buyer."

The Hardys heaved great sighs. "We're just going in circles," Joe remarked. "All the same, I'm going to check further on Clams Dagget."

"Let's radio the *Hai Hau* and find out if the fellows have seen his boat," Frank suggested.

"Good idea."

Joe soon made contact with the junk, which had not yet left Rocky Isle on its return trip to Bayport.

"Is Clams' boat around?" he asked.

"Yes, he reached here right after we did," Chet reported. "Had a full load of passengers, too. I don't know why *he's* so worried about business!"

"Well, keep an eye on him too, while you're at it," Joe ordered. "Frank and I want to ask him some questions when he lands."

"Okay, pals," Chet promised and signed off.

During the afternoon, while waiting for the junk to return, Frank and Joe phoned Dr Montrose's office and house. There was no answer from either place.

"Must be out on calls," Frank determined. "But what say we go out to his house again this evening?"

"I'm with you."

The boys sat down in the kitchen to chat with Aunt Gertrude while she gathered together the ingredients for a strawberry shortcake. They asked her what she knew about Clams Dagget.

Miss Hardy frowned. "Clams Dagget? Humph! He's an old curmudgeon!" With her usual honesty, she added, "But I'm sure he's harmless."

Joe immediately got out the dictionary to look up *curmudgeon*. He chuckled wryly as he read the definition. "Just an old crab, eh? We think he's that all right, Aunt Gertrude!"

Suddenly the short-wave radio speaker in the basement blared out. Frank dashed down to answer. Chet's voice came over loud and excited. "Frank! Joe! You'd better get down to the dock pronto! We'll land in a few minutes. Ti-Ming's causing trouble—hurry up!"

"Be right there!" Frank signed off. A minute later he and Joe were speeding towards the pier. They arrived just as the *Hai Hau* was mooring.

To their amazement, Biff and Chet led Ti-Ming off the junk with his hands tied behind his back!

·14·

The Newspaper Clue

"WHAT'S this all about?" Frank demanded as he and Joe reached the *Hai Hau*.

The dapper Ti-Ming seemed more amused than angry at his being a captive. "I am afraid you will have to ask your friends," he replied with a bland smile. "The whole situation is quite beyond my humble understanding."

"Oh yes? We caught him snooping around the junk!" Chet Morton declared furiously.

Biff, Tony and Jim vouched for this. But Ti-Ming appeared unconcerned. "I feared I had lost something," he said.

By now a crowd of curious spectators had gathered on the dock to stare at the proceedings. A policeman walked up.

"Mind if we search you?" Joe asked the Chinese.

Ti-Ming shrugged. "One can hardly resist with one's hands tied," he answered nonchalantly. "Go ahead."

Frank untied him and requested the policeman to make the search, explaining the reason. Ti-Ming's pockets contained nothing unusual and held no object belonging to the *Hai Hau*.

"We're sorry this happened, Mr Ti-Ming," Frank

apologized. "If there's any way we can make it up—"

"Please do not trouble yourselves," the Chinese assured him. "I had, otherwise, a most enjoyable boat trip."

Ti-Ming smiled suavely, bowed and walked off the pier. Now that the excitement was over, the crowd quickly dispersed. The Hardys and their friends stared at one another, nonplussed.

"Pretty slick!" Chet burst out. "But I still think that guy was looking for something on this boat."

"Maybe so," Joe said, "but we can't have him hauled in on just suspicion. He could sue us for false arrest."

Meanwhile, Clam Dagget's motor launch, the *Sandpiper*, had pulled up alongside the dock. The Hardys waited until his passengers had disembarked, then went over to speak to him.

Clams scowled. "You two again?"

"We'd like to ask you a question," Frank said.

"That ain't sayin' I'll answer it."

Frank ignored the retort and went on, "Do you own a typewriter?"

Clams' face took on a belligerent look. "Mebbe. What if I do?"

"We'd like to see it," Joe said.

"Oh, you would, would you? And what if I tell you Hardys to go jump in the bay!" the old man stormed. "I've had about enough o' your pesterin' and pryin'! What business is it o' yours whether I got a typewriter or not?"

"Just take it easy," Frank said evenly, "and read this." He handed Clams the threatening note.

"Did you write it?" Joe asked bluntly.

Clams' eyes widened as he scanned the message. "Me!" he croaked indignantly. "I never wrote no such thing!"

"All right. But maybe someone else used your typewriter." Frank paused, then added, "Unless you'd rather have the police take over."

Clams' belligerence seemed to melt away. He glanced from one to the other of the Hardys with a worried expression. "Well, all right," he grumbled. "But you're wastin' your time."

Frank and Joe motioned their friends not to wait for them, then climbed aboard the *Sandpiper*. Clams pushed off and sailed up the bay towards his shack. When they arrived, the boatman inserted a key in a rusty padlock to open the front door, and led the Hardys inside.

As Clams lighted a paraffin lamp, Frank and Joe stared about the shack curiously. It was crammed with knick-knacks and salvage items picked up during years of beachcombing. There were a boat anchor with a broken fluke, coils of hemp line, and numerous carvings of driftwood. The only furniture consisted of a bed, a potbellied stove, and a rickety table and chairs.

Joe reflected that the paraffin lamp was certainly needed, since the tiny windows were patched with cardboard, shutting out most of the daylight. Evidently the old salt was a voracious reader. Stacks of back-issue magazines lay piled about the floor.

"Well, you wanted t' see my typewriter," Clams snorted. "There it is!"

He pointed to a battered machine standing on an upended orange crate in one corner of the shack. Frank and Joe walked over to examine it. Their faces fell after one glance at the rusty antique. Not only was it much more ancient than a three-year-old model—it was *not* a Zeus!

The two boys stared at each other in chagrin. A moment later both burst out laughing.

Frank turned to Clams. "Guess we did draw a blank," he admitted.

Clams had listened in amazement, but gradually his face broke into a grin. Chuckling, he said, "Made a mistake, did you? Well, I reckon we all do, now and then!"

Relaxing, he sank down on the bed and invited the boys to make themselves at home.

"Understand, I got nothin' personal agin you two," the old beachcomber said. "But I still think you're goin' to ruin my business with that Chinese junk."

Frank and Joe tried to reassure him. They pointed out that the *Hai Hau* was a good attraction for publicizing Rocky Isle as a picnic spot. In the long run this would bring them all more customers.

"Hmm. Never thought o' that," Clams confessed. "Might be somethin' to it. I had a full boatload today, sure enough."

The Hardys offered to hike to town or catch a bus, but Clams insisted upon taking them back to the pier in the *Sandpiper*.

"Reckon we may as well bury the hatchet," he told the boys as they shook hands on parting.

"That suits us!" Joe replied with a grin. Frank agreed heartily.

Driving home, the Hardys puzzled over the reason

for Ti-Ming making the trip on the junk that day. Like their chums, Frank and Joe felt that the Chinese had a definite reason for being aboard—and it was not just to admire the scenery!

First Chin Gok had appeared in Bayport, and now the second Oriental. Certainly this was no coincidence. If the two men *were* rival leaders, they probably were transferring their war front to Bayport. But why? Was the *Hai Hau* the sole reason?

Thoughtfully the Hardys continued to High and Elm Streets. Reaching there, Joe remarked:

"You know, Frank, the solution to this whole mystery is probably right in front of our eyes, if we could only see it."

The next day was Sunday. After attending church, Frank and Joe sat in the living-room, and once more speculated on the different angles of the case. Gradually the boys became aware of an appetizing aroma wafting out from the kitchen.

"Mm, boy! Roast beef!" Frank exclaimed.

Joe perked up hungrily. "I could eat the whole piece!" he declared. "Let's see what else is on the menu!"

The boys strode out to the kitchen. Aunt Gertrude, in an apron with her sleeves pushed up, was beating whipped cream to top two large chocolate cakes. On the stove were pots of simmering vegetables and fluffy mashed potatoes. A bowl of crisp salad stood ready for the table.

"Hey! A real feast!" Joe cried. "All for us?"

"Any objection?" Aunt Gertrude retorted mysteriously.

"I'll say not. But—"

Joe's unspoken thought was drowned out by the alarm buzzers, following almost immediately by the ringing of the doorbell. Frank and Joe rushed to the front hall and opened the door to find Chet, Tony, Biff, and Jim assembled on the porch.

"What's this? A convention?" Frank asked in surprise.

"Sure—a starving one. Your aunt invited us," Chet announced. "Wow! Do I smell roast beef?"

The boys crowded inside, laughing and joking. Aunt Gertrude poked her head into the living-room to greet the newcomers. Her eyes twinkled behind her spectacles as she added to Frank and Joe:

"You two can have *your* little mysteries, so I thought I'd arrange one myself!"

"You're tops, Aunty!" Frank said, hugging her.

The boys ate heartily of the delicious dinner, Chet finishing off half of one chocolate pie. Then the brothers and their friends, in assembly-line fashion, helped Miss Hardy clear the table and wash the dishes.

When they returned to the living-room, Biff picked up the comic section of the Sunday newspaper. As he chuckled over a comic strip, Frank's eyes were caught by a headline in a report from Fremont, a town not far away.

Safe Cracked as Women Sleep

Quickly the young sleuth read the story. Dr Montrose of Bayport had treated an elderly widow, Mrs Velman, and her unmarried sister, Miss Anker, at his office. They had returned home and fallen into a deep sleep.

"According to the story told by Mrs Velman and Miss Anker," the newspaper article went on, "the women had slept for several hours.

" 'When we awoke,' Mrs Velman said, 'the safe was open, and our securities stolen!' "

Frank whistled and read the account aloud to Aunt Gertrude and the other boys. "Aunty, that sounds like your experience!"

"Are you implying," Biff spoke up, "that Dr Montrose may be the thief—or at least is in league with one?"

"I'm not accusing anyone," Frank replied, "but it's all mighty funny."

Chet spoke up. "Boy, I wish I'd come here soon enough that day to catch him!"

"I am confused," said Jim Foy. "Do you mean that Dr Montrose is paid by the burglar to put people to sleep?"

"It could be figured that way," Frank nodded.

"I'm going to find out!" Joe declared, as he jumped from his chair and dashed to the hall telephone.

Hunting an Intruder

JOE consulted the telephone directory, then dialled Mrs Velman's house. After explaining who he was and saying that his aunt had fallen asleep under similar circumstances, he found the elderly widow very co-operative.

"Did Dr Montrose give you and your sister sleeping pills?" Joe asked.

"Why—uh—yes, he did. Said we were to take them as soon as we got home. We felt fine when we woke up —that is, until we discovered the robbery."

"Is there anything else you can tell me?" the young sleuth prodded.

"I'm afraid not."

Joe said that he hoped the police would soon recover the securities, thanked her, and said goodbye. He returned to the living-room and reported what he had learned. At once Aunt Gertrude said, "Dr Montrose certainly looks suspicious."

"There are lots of reasons for talking to the doctor," said Frank. "First, he was staying at the hotel when the Zeus typewriter was stolen; second, he *could* be a thief, or in league with one; next, he advises patients, mostly elderly widows, on stock investments; and last, for a doctor who ought to be on the job he's a pretty elusive person—doesn't have a nurse or an answering service."

"I agree one hundred percent," said Joe. "Let's call on him right now!"

Aunt Gertrude held up her hand. "Not yet," she said. "I guess you've forgotten that the Forsythes, our new neighbours, are coming over to tea."

The brothers groaned, then apologized. The other boys left and in a short time Mr and Mrs Forsythe arrived with two children, a boy of ten and a girl of eight. Frank and Joe, though chafing under the delay, were polite and friendly.

A light meal was served at six o'clock. As soon as the sandwiches and ice cream were eaten, and the Forsythes had left, Frank and Joe set off for Dr Montrose's house. They would surprise the man and not give him time to hide any tell-tale evidence.

"If he's not at home," Frank said, "we'll look around the grounds and see if we can learn anything to connect him with the mystery."

As on their previous call, the Hardys found the chain across the entrance driveway, so they parked on the public road. The boys walked up the path through the wooded approach and rang the doorbell. No one answered.

After ringing several more times, with no response, Frank muttered, "Looks as though he's not at home."

"Or else just not seeing callers," Joe added.

Disappointed, the boys made their way to the outside of the house, looking for discarded letters or other possible incriminating clues. As they passed a pair of tall french windows opening off the ground floor, Joe seized his brother's arm.

"Wait!" he whispered. "I think someone's in there!" He pointed to one of the windows.

Frank also caught a fleeting glimpse of a tall figure moving about inside. The two boys silently went up and peered through the glass. The next instant both stiffened as a steely voice behind them rang out:

"Why are you two spying here?" The boys whirled about. There stood Dr Montrose, wearing a hat and scowling accusingly. But his harsh look turned to a smile of welcome as he recognized them.

"Why, Frank and Joe Hardy!" he exclaimed. "This *is* a surprise! What brings you here? Is your aunt ill again?"

"Oh, no, she's better, thank you," Joe replied. "We came here to ask you about something. When you didn't answer the bell, we decided just to look around."

"I see. Well, come inside," the doctor urged cordially.

As the two boys accompanied him into the house, they glanced at each other, thinking, "He's not acting like a guilty person!"

Dr Montrose clicked on a light and laid his hat on the table in the wide hall. He invited them to follow him into a living-room to sit down.

Frank and Joe glanced around, trying not to appear too curious. The atmosphere was musty, as if the whole house needed an airing, and the gilt-trimmed plush furniture looked old and very worn. The windows were hung with heavy red draperies.

"I suppose you're wondering why we were looking in the windows," Frank said to the doctor. "The fact is, when no one answered our ring we assumed you were out. But we thought we saw someone inside."

"It surprised us," Joe added, "because we understood you live alone."

"That's right." Dr Montrose nodded. "No one else is here."

Joe purposely put on a puzzled look. "That's strange," he insisted. "I'm positive I caught a glimpse of a person moving around. You don't suppose it was a burglar?"

The doctor laughed, evidently undisturbed. "It was probably only an illusion caused by the shadows. Well, perhaps I'd better look around—just to make sure."

Frank seized the opening. "We'll help," he offered. "It might be safer with three of us, if there *is* an intruder."

"Hmm, certainly. That's very kind."

Both boys thought they now detected a certain reluctance in the doctor's manner. Nevertheless, he led them through the various rooms on the ground floor. Apparently the mansion had not received a thorough house cleaning in a long time. Cobwebs hung from the ceiling and much of the furniture was still draped with white dust covers. The once-expensive carpets were threadbare and soiled.

After checking the huge, old-fashioned kitchen and peering into the butler's pantry, Montrose led them back to the sweeping spiral staircase in the main hallway.

"We'll take a glance upstairs," he murmured.

The dried-out wooden steps creaked underfoot.

"Boy, this place seems a million years old!" Joe whispered to his brother.

The searchers looked into all the bedrooms, one by one, and then into two enormous antique bathrooms with tubs mounted on ball-claw feet. The white tile floors were chipped.

Next the doctor mounted a narrow rickety staircase that led upwards to the attic storage rooms. Frank and Joe followed. The musty staleness that assailed their lungs caused them to cough.

"I dare say we could do with some air conditioning up here," Dr Montrose apologized with an affable smile as they reached the hot, stifling loft.

Frank and Joe agreed wholeheartedly. Dr Montrose switched on an overhead bulb, revealing an assortment of discarded articles. There were several battered trunks, a rusty bird-cage, and piles of yellowing newspapers. Everything was coated with a thick layer of dust.

"No intruder has been up here or we'd see his footprints." The doctor chuckled.

Although the brothers had to agree, Frank and Joe still looked behind every piece big enough to conceal a person—or a typewriter. They found nothing suspicious.

When they returned to the ground floor, Frank pointed to a latched door at one end of the hall.

"We haven't looked in there," he said.

"Just a small cupboard," Dr Montrose replied casually. "No one could hide in it."

He proceeded down the spiral stairway to the ground floor, with Joe following. Frank, lingering behind, decided to check the cupboard himself.

Moving quickly down the hall, he opened the door and peered inside. The next instant a tall figure loomed up out of the pitch-dark space.

Before Frank could take action, he was seized by powerful hands. The boy started to yell, then the sound was choked off by his assailant's crushing grip. The man was almost a head taller than Frank, and in the dim light of the hallway it was impossible to see his face.

Frank fought furiously to free himself. The locked pair swayed and stumbled in a wordless struggle. Then one hand of Frank's opponent grasped the boy's throat and banged his head against the cupboard door jamb.

The impact sent a flash of pain shooting through Frank's skull. With a groan, he blacked out!

· 16 ·

Signals

MEANWHILE, Joe and Dr Montrose had reached the ground floor. It was a moment before they realized that Frank was not behind them. Then they heard sounds of a commotion upstairs.

"Hey! What's going on?" Joe cried. He ran back to the staircase and dashed up two steps at a time. The doctor followed, pantingly urging caution.

By the time they reached the first floor, the scuffling noises had ceased. Frank was nowhere in sight.

"Frank!" Joe yelled. "Hey, Frank! Where are you?"

The cupboard door stood ajar. Dr Montrose switched on the hall light and Joe peered inside. The place was empty.

"He must be up here somewhere!" Joe exclaimed frantically.

They peered into every bedroom and both bathrooms, but found no trace of the other Hardy boy. Then Joe noticed a laundry chute in one wall of the hallway and yanked it open.

"It leads down to the cellar," Dr Montrose explained. "But surely he didn't—"

Without waiting to hear more, Joe dashed downstairs again. "Which way to the cellar?" he shouted over his shoulder.

"Through the kitchen!" Dr Montrose answered, hastening down the steps behind him.

Joe sped on and descended the cellar steps, pausing only long enough to flick on the light switch. The basement was like a huge, cobwebby tomb.

Only a single light bulb was working, but Joe noticed a wooden partition at one end of the basement with the words, LAUNDRY ROOM, in faded paint on the door. He struggled with the latch for a moment, then yanked the door open.

"*Frank!*" he cried in mingled relief and alarm.

His brother lay stunned at the bottom of the laundry chute. Joe slipped one arm under Frank's shoulders and raised him to a half-sitting position. In doing so, Joe felt a sizeable bump on the back of his brother's head.

Dr Montrose had arrived on the scene by this time and hastily examined Frank.

"Frank's had a nasty blow," he murmured, "but I think he's coming round."

After the doctor and Joe had chafed the victim's wrists for a few moments, Frank opened his eyes and groaned.

"O-oh, my head! . . . Wh-where am I?"

"Down in the cellar, pal," Joe replied. "Take it easy for a bit, and then tell us what happened."

After collecting his wits, Frank related how he had looked in the cupboard and been taken off guard by his huge assailant. "Where is he now?"

"Not upstairs, that's certain," Dr Montrose pointed out.

Joe pointed to an open window above the laundry tubs. "That's how the guy escaped. After he dumped

Frank into the chute, he must have slid down behind him and ducked out."

The doctor looked at the boys blankly. "But what did he want? There is nothing of great value in the house."

The Hardys exchanged puzzled glances. They were wondering the same thing. It occurred to both boys that the intruder evidently had some knowledge of the layout of the house.

Dr Montrose and Joe assisted Frank upstairs and made him comfortable in a lounge chair. Here the doctor gave him a whiff of spirits of ammonia and a glass of water. In a few minutes the young sleuth felt fully recovered, except for a throbbing bump on his head.

"I think you'd better call the police, Dr Montrose," Joe suggested.

"Yes, I'll do that, but it seems foolish if the fellow didn't take anything. Probably he was just a tramp who broke in to get some food. I'll take a look."

The doctor hurried off to the kitchen but returned in a minute. "That was the answer, all right. The fellow took a lot of food."

Dr Montrose dismissed the subject, then asked why the boys had come.

"On several counts, but we'll make it brief," Frank replied. "First, a friend of ours is looking for a certain kind of typewriter that isn't for sale around here. We heard that you have one."

"A typewriter?" The doctor's piercing eyes glinted with surprise. "Why, no—no indeed. I've never thought of having one."

"Next," Frank went on, "we've been tremendously

interested in what happened at Mrs Velman's home. We'd like to hear your theory on it."

Dr Montrose smiled. "I'm afraid that I haven't any," he replied.

"But you did tell Mrs Velman and her sister to take sleeping pills right before the robbery!"

The doctor frowned. "I do not like your insinuations," he said darkly. "I know nothing about the robbery." He suddenly arose, indicating that the interview was at an end. The boys said goodnight and left.

As soon as their convertible was rolling homewards, Frank said, "Well, do you think our suspicions about the doctor should be washed out?"

"No indeed," Joe declared. "I'm sure he's mixed up in this mystery somehow."

"You found something?" Frank asked.

In response Joe reached into his pocket. "Look at this. It was on the floor in the laundry room."

He held out a gold cuff link, set with a bluish amber tiger, and on the reverse side were the Oriental characters meaning Hong Kong.

"It's the mate to the one Iola found at the cave!" Frank exclaimed. "You think this is Dr Montrose's?"

"Could be," Joe answered. "Or at least it belonged to the man who attacked you, and he was no housebreaker. He's a pal of Dr Montrose!"

"A long shot," Frank replied, then smiled. "But a good one. That guy could even be the safe-cracker!"

"The question is, could he be Chinese and what's Dr Montrose's part in all this?" Frank queried.

"And I'd like to know," Joe put in, "is he one of the people interested in the *Hai Hau*? Or, if Dr Montrose owns the cuff links, is he tied up in any way with one or another of the rival groups, and why?"

"And, Joe, don't forget that Dad said the Chameleon was looking for cuff links like those we have. That could mean the owner might lead us to that man Balarat."

"First we must prove who the owner is," said Joe.

"I think we should check on the doctor's credentials," Frank declared.

Joe concurred. "For a starter, let's find out if that fancy diploma in his office is on the level. Let's see. It was Ardvor College."

The next morning there was just time enough for Joe to write a letter of inquiry to Ardvor College. Frank, meanwhile, phoned Chief Collig to brief him on all the Hardys' suspicions up to date regarding Dr Montrose.

"I'll start investigating the doctor at once," the officer promised. "Your story is amazing. And I'll get in touch with your father if you're in a hurry."

"Thanks."

Joe licked the envelope of his letter and applied an airmail and a special-delivery stamp.

"Hey, come on! It's almost ten o'clock!" Frank urged, with a glance at his wrist watch. "We can drop the letter off on our way to the pier!"

The *Hai Hau* was ready to pull out as the Hardys arrived on the pier. They climbed aboard and Joe went forward to help Chet with the bowlines.

Two last-minute passengers, a husband and wife, showed up a moment later, breathless and clutching picnic bags. Biff and Frank took their fares and assisted them to embark.

"Another full boatload!" Biff beamed.

Frank grinned with satisfaction. "Nice going. Well, let's shove off!"

The day's cruises went off without a hitch. Secretly Frank and Joe kept wishing that they could have worked on the mystery, and radioed Aunt Gertrude several times for news. None came and finally the brothers arrived home at dinnertime.

Later that evening they were talking to Aunt Gertrude about Dr Montrose when the alarm buzzers sounded. The visitors proved to be Biff Hooper and Tony Prito. Both were highly excited.

"What's up?" Joe demanded.

"Plenty!" Tony was panting for breath. "You remember that yarn Clams Dagget told us about seeing lights on Rocky Isle?"

"Sure. What about them?" Frank said. "They've been seen again?"

"Yes. This time by Biff and me. We were out in my *Napoli* and spotted those lights ourselves! They were blinking on and off, as if someone was sending a message in secret code!"

The Cliffside Cave

"Wow!" Joe cried. "Let's get going, fellows! Now's our chance to find out who's sending secret signals from Rocky Isle!"

"We'll have to wait for Chet and Jim," Biff put in. "They'll be right over."

"Okay. We can all go in the *Sleuth*," Frank said.

Chet's noisy jalopy pulled up outside a few moments later. Jim was with him. The other boys rushed out, some sliding into the Hardys' convertible, the others into Chet's "hot rod". They drove to the town pier.

"Let's make sure the *Hai Hau*'s all right before we leave," Frank suggested.

The boys found that Detective Smuff and Patrolman Con Riley had been assigned as police guards for the junk. Seeing the pair, Joe and Frank looked at one another. The two officers were not known as the most astute men on the force.

"Guess Chief Collig didn't have any others to spare," Joe remarked with a shrug.

The junk's owners went on and hurried to the boathouse where the *Sleuth* was berthed. Within minutes the craft was kicking up a frothy wake in the moonlight as the group sped out of the bay and neared Rocky Isle.

132 THE MYSTERY OF THE CHINESE JUNK

It loomed up as a black mass on the horizon, with its lighthouse beacon sweeping the darkness at one-minute intervals. At the moment there was no sign of the blinking signals on the opposite side of the island.

"Maybe we've missed the senders," Frank said glumly to his boatmates. He was at the wheel of the *Sleuth*.

A second later a light suddenly gleamed from the western cliff!

"There it goes!" Joe exclaimed, watching intently so that he could translate the message. The light shone steadily for a few moments, then winked on and off rapidly. "That wasn't Morse code—or International!" Joe added tensely.

Jim Foy nodded. "It must be a secret one!" His companions agreed.

The light disappeared as they moved closer. Frank had fixed its approximate position in mind, and steered towards the jumbled mass of rock that soared upwards from the island's northern shore.

"It's starting again!" Biff exclaimed. Once, twice, three times the blinking signal stabbed the darkness. Still it made no sense to the boys.

"If only we can get close enough to see who's sending!" Joe muttered.

He broke off as the group became aware of the sudden drone of a powerful boat engine. The sound was coming from the direction of the island, but the boys could detect no running lights. Seconds later, they could make out the dim form of a large motorboat. It was zooming straight towards the *Sleuth*!

"It'll ram us broadside!" Chet cried.

"No, it won't!" Frank said grimly, setting his jaw.

He tooted the *Sleuth*'s horn, and the sound echoed back from the cliff. Still the darkened boat aimed for the boys. Frank turned the wheel to give the other craft plenty of room. It veered, still obstructing the *Sleuth*.

"That pilot's crazy!" Tony cried out, then yelled, "Look where you're going!"

The oncoming motorboat continued to change course whenever Frank did. Finally he decided on a daring move to outwit the person determined to crash into them.

Frank steeled his nerve and held course and speed as the other boat bore down on the Hardy craft. Then, at the very last second, he revved the *Sleuth*'s engine and threw the wheel hard over!

With an earsplitting din, the big motorboat hurtled past, missing them by inches! The *Sleuth* heeled crazily aport in its wake.

Chet was trembling like a leaf. Biff, Tony and Jim gave weak gasps of relief. Joe felt cold trickles of perspiration run down his back.

"Terrific, Frank! You rate a medal for fast thinking!" Joe called, as his brother sped on. This time the motorboat did not come in pursuit.

"What was that guy's idea?" Biff asked. "In fact, there were two men in that boat. Wonder who they were."

"I think they have something to do with the signalling and were trying to scare us away from Rocky Isle," Frank suggested.

"Then that's all the more reason for going there," Joe determined.

"I'll say," Tony broke in angrily. "How about our finding those guys and asking what their murderous scheme was all about?"

"Oh, no!" Chet spoke up. "I aim to stay in one piece now that they're gone. Let's just take a look at the cliff and call it quits."

"That seems wise," Jim Foy said softly.

Frank headed towards the cliff once more, watching intently for any sign of another attack. But the place was quiet.

Suddenly lights flashed again high up on the cliff. They seemed to be coming from some recessed ledge, just below the craggy out-thrust of the cliff's overhanging brow. Then the signals blacked out abruptly.

"Slow down!" Joe called. "Think that motorboat could be luring us into a trap?"

"Maybe. Fellows, get out your flashlights and beam them around."

His companions did as directed. No boat or waiting figures were to be seen. The signalling had stopped. The boys held a hurried conference and concluded that by the time they could climb the cliff the mysterious signal sender would have vanished.

"Let's go home," Chet pleaded, yawning, but still sweeping the cliff with his light. "I—" The sleepy boy suddenly jumped up and cried out, "Hey, that looks like the entrance to a cave up there!"

His friends stared at the spot on which the beam of his flashlight was trained. "Oh, man, am I ever going spelunking in there! . . . No, not tonight," Chet added quickly as he saw the look of amazement on the other boys' faces.

Since there seemed to be no reason for remaining longer, Frank headed the *Sleuth* towards Bayport. Conversation revolved around the lights and the cave. "There might be a connection," Chet offered.

"And," Biff drawled, "those signals might just be on the level and have something to do with the Coast Guard."

Joe grinned. "More likely those phoney coast-guards."

The *Sleuth* ploughed on. As it came in sight of the *Hai Hau*, Jim Foy cried out, "Good grief! What's up?"

The dock's floodlight illuminated a strange scene. Figures could be seen in wild commotion on the junks' fore and afterdecks!

Frank brought the *Sleuth* to the dock in a hurry and leaped out.

"It's the Chinese!" Tony cried out, as he and the others raced aboard the *Hai Hau*.

In the junk's stern, George Ti-Ming was exchanging fisticuffs with two other Chinese, while Officer Con Riley fought to separate them. The Hardys recognized Ti-Ming's opponents as two of the men who had wanted to buy the *Hai Hau* in Staten Island.

In the forepart of the craft, another hand-to-hand battle was going on. Frank made out the huge figure of Chin Gok locked in combat with two smaller adversaries. The face of one was contorted with pain. Detective Smuff was trying to pry them apart, and in doing so, was catching the brunt of their blows.

Frank waded into the fray on the foredeck. He yanked Chin Gok round by one arm and dealt him a strong right to the jaw. Chin Gok's eyes went glassy and he reeled back against the cabin wall.

Tony, meanwhile, had shot a short, jarring left chop to the ribs of another of the battlers, who had not yet recovered from the surprise of this new and unexpected intervention. Jim's fists, too, were dealing out equal punishment to the other Chinese.

Joe, Biff and Chet were busy with the fighters in the stern sheets. Within minutes, the battle of the *Hai Hau* had been brought under control and all six of the bruised and panting Chinese were only too willing to subside.

"What was this fracas all about? And why here on the *Hai Hau*?" Frank demanded.

Smuff and Riley looked shamefaced, and the latter said, "This guy"—he pointed to Ti-Ming— "came aboard to look around with a couple of friends. I didn't see any harm in that."

"Riley's telling you right," Smuff spoke up. "Then these other guys arrived with the same story. First thing we knew a fight started."

At that moment a police car raced up to the pier. Chief Collig and two other officers stepped out and raced on to the junk.

"It's all right, Chief," Smuff spoke up. "Riley and I have the situation under control. Pretty bad fight."

The chief looked hard at his men and said that a bystander had telephoned headquarters about the fight. To the Chinese, Chief Collig said:

"You're all under arrest. Do you want to talk here or down at headquarters?"

Chin Gok and his two henchmen sullenly made it

plain they would not talk anywhere. But Ti-Ming said he welcomed the chance to clear himself.

"I am not guilty of any lawbreaking," he began. "I am a private detective. I go from place to place to get evidence on smuggling."

Frank and Joe were thunderstruck. A detective! And he solved smuggling cases!

Would Ti-Ming's story clear up the mystery of the Chinese junk?

· 18 ·

Legend of Treasure

To VERIFY his story, Ti-Ming produced a New York private detective's licence and several letters from Hong Kong. They identified not only him without a doubt, but the friends with him as well.

"Why didn't you tell the police all this when you came here?" Chief Collig demanded.

"Because I was not yet sure whether the *Hai Hau* was the stolen junk I was looking for; whether Chin Gok's gang or someone else had smuggled goods into this country on it; and whether he had learned of a certain secret hidden aboard the junk. Until I was, I thought it wiser to keep my true identity under cover."

Ti-Ming explained that six junks similar to the *Hai Hau* had been stolen in Hong Kong, probably by Chin Gok, painted, and given new figureheads and names. It was thought they had been shipped to various ports of the world, all with smuggled goods aboard. One of these boats belonged to a friend of Ti-Ming's.

"In Hong Kong," the Chinese detective went on, "a story was told by a workman that on one of the junks an ancient clue to a great fortune could be found. This workman was injured and before dying told this much but could never finish the story. As far as is known, no one has learned the secret."

Ti-Ming smiled. "Naturally my friend hoped the secret was hidden in his boat."

"What is the fortune?" Joe asked eagerly.

Ti-Ming did not reply.

"You needn't answer that question now," Collig said. "Go on with your story."

The detective bowed slightly. "My friend heard that a shipment of boats had gone from Hong Kong to New York and asked me to investigate. The *Hai Hau* was the only used junk among them, and I am sure from certain features and other marks that it is my friend's boat. To avoid confusion and publicity, I offered to buy it. When these honourable boys refused to sell, I followed them to Bayport and tried to continue my search without their suspecting me. But they are very wise young men."

Despite the compliment to them, the Hardys and their friends exchanged worried glances. "Then it is true we bought stolen property!" Frank remarked solemnly.

"I am afraid so," Ti-Ming replied. But smiling, he added, "The rightful owner authorized me, after I notified him of my find, to say that you may keep the *Hai Hau* until the end of summer, but in the meantime I am to be permitted to continue my hunt for the clue to the fortune."

The Hardys looked towards Chief Collig, who gave the Chinese a quick answer. "You may search only with a police escort, Mr Ti-Ming, and anything you find will be kept by me until we have further proof of ownership."

Ti-Ming nodded. "That is very fair. And now, if you

will excuse me, my friends and I will say good evening to you gentlemen. I will return in the morning, when I will search for the valuable clue to the fortune."

Chin Gok and his two henchmen glared in hate after the departing Chinese. Still refusing to admit anything, they were led off to the Bayport jail. Chief Collig asked Frank and Joe to follow. Surprised and wondering, they said goodnight to their friends and followed in the convertible.

At police headquarters Chief Collig attempted once more to make his prisoners talk. But he was unable to extract any information from the three men.

"Empty their pockets," he ordered a guard.

Aside from knives carried by two of the men, nothing incriminating was found until they searched Chin Gok. A turnout of his pockets revealed a blue amber tiger gem!

Joe pounced on it. "Chief! This is like the jewels in the cuff links!"

Collig's eyes narrowed. "So you were the man who threw Frank Hardy down the laundry chute! All right, speak up! What have you got to say for yourself?"

Chin Gok's long face twisted into a sneer, but he said nothing.

"Okay, if they won't talk, lock 'em all up!" Collig growled. "Chin Gok, we'll hold you for assault on Frank Hardy. The others will be charged with disturbing the peace while we make a further investigation."

After the three Chinese had been led away, Chief Collig took the brothers into his office. "Get ready for a bombshell," he said. "Dr Montrose has disappeared!"

"What!"

"After you gave us the tip on him, my men went to call on him. When they found his office locked, we became suspicious and broke in. Everything but the heavy furniture was gone."

Joe whistled, and Frank said, "Yes, go on. Then you went to his house?"

"Right away. Same thing there." Collig smiled. "I guess you boys broke the case of a fake-doctor thief."

"You mean there weren't two men working together?" Joe exclaimed.

Chief Collig rubbed his chin. "On that score I'm not sure. Montrose may have returned to the victim's houses himself and stolen their securities, or he may have a pal take them."

"Chin Gok, perhaps?" Frank suggested.

The chief shrugged. "I hadn't thought of that until the cuff-link angle came up. The point now is to find Dr Montrose. Well, boys, thanks for your help. And if you get any leads, let me know."

"We sure will," Frank promised and with a grin added, "If Chin Gok talks, call us, please."

"I'll do that. By the way, I never did get in touch with your father. He was always out."

The Hardys left for home, conversing on the way about each detail of the mystery, "I'm beginning to reconstruct things this way," said Frank. "When Dr Montrose left our house, after Aunt Gertrude was getting sleepy, he slipped the lock on the front door. He took Mrs Witherspoon home and returned to open Dad's safe. Something frightened him and he ran off in a hurry, leaving the front door open. Then Chet came along."

"Sounds good," Joe remarked. "But if he steals securities whenever he gets a chance, why didn't he take the ones in our safe?"

"He didn't want that particular job to look like a robbery," Frank answered. "All he wanted was Dad's file on the Chameleon."

Joe's eyes opened wide. "Are you trying to tell me you think Montrose is the Chameleon?"

"I am." Frank gave a loud sigh. "And we let him slip right through our fingers. The Chameleon is sure a perfect name for that guy! He managed to fool other doctors in town evidently."

Joe said he thought they should phone their father at once, so as soon as the boys reached home, Frank put in the call. His brother, meanwhile, gave Aunt Gertrude an account of the evening's adventures.

"Dr Montrose!" she cried out. "And he seemed like such a gentleman! So he's not, eh? Then he ought to be tarred and feathered when they catch him. The idea of giving people sleeping pills and then robbing them!"

"Take it easy, Aunty," Joe advised. "Remember, we haven't proved a thing yet."

By this time Frank had made the connection to California and in a moment his father came on the phone. Mr Hardy listened in amazement to the story and his sons' deductions. Then he said:

"One of my secret findings contained in the Chameleon's files was that he had read a great deal about medicine and learned enough to pose as a doctor. But the last place I'd expect to find him practising would be Bayport! At the time the file on Balarat was taken from my safe, I had just received a good lead that he was out here, and I figured some associate of his had opened the safe."

Mr Hardy went on to say that the ex-convict might remain in hiding for some time, now that he knew his latest role as a doctor had been detected. "But keep your eyes open, Frank, and Joe too," the ace sleuth advised. "I will fly home tomorrow with Mother to take up the hunt."

After Frank put the phone down, Aunt Gertrude looked hard at him, then said crisply, "Not one more bit of mystery tonight for either of you boys. You both look as white and tired as if you'd been through an epidemic!"

"An epidemic of clues," Joe quipped, but he and Frank were glad to climb into bed and were asleep in a few minutes.

The following morning was bright and warm and the Hardys looked forward to a full passenger list for the *Hai Hau.* They found Aunt Gertrude busy in the kitchen taking muffins from the oven.

"Wow! What a breakfast!" said Joe. "Here's a kiss for the cook." He planted one on her cheek.

"Good morning, Aunty," Frank added, putting an arm around her.

The wall phone in the kitchen rang. Joe picked it up and listened for a moment, then burst out:

"What! Chin Gok and the other two prisoners have escaped, you say, Chief?"

· 19 ·

Sleuths in Danger

FRANK, JOE and Aunt Gertrude were stunned by Chief Collig's report that the three Chinese prisoners had broken out of jail.

"Somebody helped them," Aunt Gertrude declared firmly.

"He sure did," Joe agreed. "The chief said someone slugged the jailer and opened the cell they were in. The fellow was masked and as slick as they come. Nobody saw him sneak in."

Frank gazed into space. "I wonder where the bunch of escapees went. They must be in hiding. Maybe—"

"Maybe what?" Aunt Gertrude asked.

Her nephew merely smiled and she knew his idea was still in a nebulous state. He would tell her later when it was fully formulated. As the brothers drove down to the *Hai Hau* to help with the day's run, Frank said:

"Joe, I was thinking of that cave on Rocky Isle and those blinking lights. It's just possible Dr Montrose is hiding out there."

"And perhaps Chin Gok and his pals?" Joe queried.

"Yes. Let's take a look and if we see any of them we'll radio the police."

At the pier Frank and Joe found Chet with his spelunking gear, ready to explore the cave. But when the stout boy heard of the jail break and Frank's supposition that the wanted men might be hiding there, he looked worried.

"I don't know that I'll explore, fellows. You can't move fast in this gear and I sure couldn't run if I had to."

"Well, suit yourself," said Joe.

Several picnickers had already gathered. Among them were Callie Shaw and Iola Morton. The girls had brought a basket of food, a portable record player, and a beach bag containing towels and bathing suits.

"Hey! Look who's here!" Joe cried out.

"Be our guests!" Frank invited. "We'll reserve deluxe seats right here with the crew—no charge!"

The two girls dimpled into pleased smiles but insisted upon paying their own fares.

Laughter and banter continued as the junk cruised out of the harbour. Then Iola turned on a new hit record.

"Too bad there's not enough room to dance," she sighed. "Let's all sing instead!"

Everyone joined in the chorus, drowning out the voice on the record. Biff sang slightly off key.

"Hey! Those pipes of yours are rusty!" Tony joked and held up an oilcan. "Try some."

Presently the radio connected with the Hardy home signalled and Aunt Gertrude's voice came on. Frank turned down the volume so that only the young sleuths and their friends could hear her.

"A phone message just came from Ardvor College,"

she said. "Dr Montrose was never a student there and the president is very upset by his claims. I've notified Chief Collig. Anything else you want me to do?"

"Not now. And thanks a million, Aunty," said Frank. "Over and out." Turning to his friends he added, "If we needed extra proof about that phoney, we have it now!"

As soon as the junk was tied up at the wharf, its passengers trooped ashore and headed for the beach. Frank told the girls that he and Joe were going to the cave, but did not give the reason. Chet decided to don his spelunking helmet and accompany them. Tony, Biff and Jim would go back to Bayport for the second load of passengers.

The Hardys and their stout chum tramped across the island. Reaching the park keeper's house, they stopped to ask Dave Roberts if he had seen any blinking lights or cliff climbers on the northern end of Rocky Isle.

"No," he replied, and the boys went on.

The trio skirted the rocks along the shore and half an hour later started up the cliffside. Twenty minutes of scaling brought them to the mouth of the cave.

"If those jailbirds climbed up these rocks, they sure made it hard for themselves," said Chet, puffing. "I don't believe they're here."

"Just the same, we'd better talk in whispers," Frank recommended.

The three boys pressed forward into the gloomy cave. They had barely entered when several rocks near the opening went clattering down the hillside. The vibration loosened a massive chunk of limestone hanging from the cave ceiling.

It plunged straight towards Joe's head!

"Look out!" Chet yelled.

Joe dived clear in the nick of time, aided by a lightning grab from Frank. The huge chunk of limestone smashed on the spot where Joe had just been standing! All three boys were showered with whitish dust and rock fragments.

"Whew! It—it was almost curtains that time!" Joe's voice came in a weak whisper. He lay sprawled full length on the cave floor.

Frank helped him to his feet. "Are you all right?"

"I guess so—thanks to you two!" Joe gulped. "Boy, if you hadn't yelled, Chet—"

"Now you know why I wear this miner's hat!" Chet replied.

Suddenly Frank said, "We certainly made a noisy entrance. If anyone's hiding, we probably alerted him."

Joe nodded. "That gives him the advantage. We'd better proceed with the utmost caution and not get trapped."

As they advanced, the boys beamed their flashlights in every direction. Presently they found themselves in an enormous room.

Pearly terraces rimmed the walls, extending far back into the cliff. Glittering calcite icicles hung from the ceiling.

"This is a *living* cave," Chet whispered. "That means there's always water seepage going on. It builds these queer, shiny formations. When the seepage dries up, the rock gets dull and crumbly, and the cave becomes dead."

Chet now lit his helmet lamp and the boys proceeded

deeper into the cave. The floor became more rugged, forcing them to pick their way along cautiously.

The path they were taking gradually sloped upwards. Another branch of the cavern, opening on their right, seemed to lead down towards the base of the cliff. The boys hesitated, uncertain which way to go.

"In the daytime those men would be more likely to hide down below the top of the cliff," Frank suggested.

The others nodded, and the boys pushed on into the right-hand cavern. Here, the "icicles" increased in size to huge spearlike stalactites. Here and there similarly shaped stalagmites jutted upwards from the floor. Sometimes the twin formations joined in glistening pillars or columns.

"Just think! This was all done by water dripping slowly for hundreds of years," Chet marvelled.

"What a spectacle!" Frank whispered. "This place ought to be opened up to the public."

Most eye-stopping of all was a frozen cascade that had formed over a ledge, like a miniature Niagara of stone. It glistened with a fairy-like brilliance in the glow of the flashlights and lamp.

"Chet, this is super. I'll never make fun of your spelunking again!" Joe declared in a low, awed voice.

To add to the beauty, some of the deposits were tinted orange, red and brown. Chet explained that this was due to iron oxide and other minerals in the dripping water.

As the boys continued downwards into the cliff, their body heat caused wispy fog to form in the cool, damp air. Suddenly Frank halted and listened.

"I thought I heard a voice."

The boys tiptoed ahead and presently the twisting passageway opened into a larger cavern. In the middle lay a huge pool, its surface covered with a thick scum of green algae and slime. A slight movement of the water indicated that the pool was being fed from some underground source. The ocean?

"Look!" Frank whispered excitedly, pointing across the pool.

Joe and Chet swung their lights towards the spot. Revealed was a typewriter with the name Zeus on it. No doubt the stolen one! Next to it was a low table on which stood stacks of what looked like bonds or other financial certificates. On top of these was a foot-square bamboo box with Oriental characters on it.

"We've found it!" Joe gasped. "This *is* the thieves' and smugglers' hi—"

His words ended in a groan as a hard object crashed against his skull! Before Frank and Chet could turn round, they too were struck down from behind. All three sank into blackness.

When the Hardys and Chet regained consciousness, it was like waking to a flickering nightmare. The boys could feel ropes biting into their wrists and ankles. They were bound and propped against one wall of the cavern, now lit by carbide lamps. Frank's watch revealed that three hours had gone by since the boys had left the dock.

Frank was first to collect his wits fully. Then Joe and Chet slowly brought their eyes to a focus on four figures leering down at them; Dr Montrose, Chin Gok and two rough-looking men in seamen's dungarees.

"The phoney coastguards!" Frank said grimly.

"Yes," one of them replied, "but you'll never live to report where we are." He laughed scornfully.

Frank took a deep breath. "In that case, you won't mind clearing up the mystery first," he said, playing for time. "Dr Montrose, we know you're Balarat, the Chameleon. You're wanted on various charges, including the display of a fake diploma. But what is your connection with Chin Gok?"

"I'll answer that," the Chinese spoke up and gave a harsh, leering laugh. "Balarat and I are new in our acquaintance but already very good friends. He helped us slip out of jail. The doctor and I thank the Hardy boys for our first meeting. It was at your house."

"Our house!" Frank and Joe gasped.

Chin Gok grew voluble. "It was quite by accident," he confessed. "I entered your home one morning to search for any data you might have picked up regarding the *Hai Hau*. Incidentally, it was my esteemed self who spoke that warning over the radio. That was between the doctor's first and second visits that day. I followed him upstairs and watched him open your father's safe." The Chinese smiled. "I might have blackmailed him, but when Montrose saw the unusual cuff links I was wearing, he recognized them as part of a smuggled shipment of amber. As payment for his silence, I gave them to him. Then we decided to join forces and outwit the Hardy family!"

"Chin Gok," Joe said, "did you steal all six junks in Hong Kong and secrete smuggled goods aboard, part of it bluish amber tigers? And did you have the junks shipped to foreign ports where you picked up the loot and sold it?"

"True," Chin Gok replied. "I have sold everything, except the valuable bluish ambers in the bamboo box, with the help of Dr Montrose." A self-satisfied smile played over the smuggler's face. "Friends took care of five junks. I came to New York because I was particularly interested in the boat I repainted and put the mandarin figurehead on, and gave the name *Hai Hau*."

Chin Gok spoke proudly. After a pause he went on, "I had some of my men ruin the junk's engine and later attack you boys in Chinatown. After that, they put a hole in the junk to discourage you from keeping the *Hai Hau*."

"Did they also slug the dock watchman and make a search aboard?" Joe asked.

Chin Gok nodded. "They almost got the *Hai Hau* away from you one night out on the Shore Road. And they did scare you with a warning note."

Frank looked hard at the man. "You're the one who pretended to be stooped like Clams Daggett when we saw you leave Montrose's house."

"Yes."

Frank turned to Dr Montrose. "And you lost one cuff link when you met Chin Gok at the cave and dropped the other in your basement."

"You are right. It must have dropped out of my shirt pocket when I bent down to get something out of a toolbox. Incidentally, I was a prowler at your house twice."

"Did you ever shoot at the *Hai Hau*?" Joe asked.

Butler said, "I took a practice shot once."

Chin Gok broke in. "But our work is not finished. For my part, I haven't yet found the clue to the *Hai*

Hau's treasure, but I will! You will not stop me!"

"What do you mean? What are you going to do to us?" Chet quavered.

"Butler and Burns," Dr Montrose spoke up, looking towards the two sham coastguards, "you tell them."

The one named Butler burst into harsh, mocking laughter. "See that pool? Well, that's where you're headin'. We're goin' to throw all three o' you boys, tied up just like you are, into this bottomless hole!"

· 20 ·

Underground Battle

UNAWARE of the grim happenings under the cliff, two groups of the *Hai Hau*'s passengers were thoroughly enjoying themselves. To pass the time, Biff, Tony and Jim began searching the junk again for a clue to the treasure. After a dip in the surf, Iola and Callie strolled back to the wharf.

"Find anything?" Iola asked.

"No," Biff replied.

"Let's all look," Callie suggested. "Maybe we can surprise Frank and Joe with a clue!"

The five friends joined in the hunt. Tony perched himself in the bow, with one leg swung over the side. He scowled thoughtfully as his eyes roved the hull of the *Hai Hau.*

Could the clue to the fortune be hidden somewhere on the *outside* of the junk? Absent-mindedly he pressed one of the glass eyes in the figurehead. To his surprise, it pushed inwards! Tony gave a yell that brought the others running.

A secret panel had slid open on the inner side of the bulwark!

"I've found something!" Excitedly he reached into the small compartment and pulled out a bamboo tube. He peered inside it and, as everyone watched breathlessly, extracted a parchment scroll. When unrolled, it proved to be a faded, yellow map labelled with Cantonese characters.

"A treasure map!" Jim Foy exclaimed. "It tells where there are rich mines of bluish amber!"

A hasty conference followed. Both Tony and Biff felt that they should inform the Hardys and Chet at once. The girls agreed, but asked Jim to remain with them and help guard the treasure map.

Iola tucked the scroll into her swimming bag. "Let's radio the Coast Guard to come over here," she said. "I'll feel much safer."

"Okay! Let's go!" Tony urged Biff.

The two set off across the island, scrambled up the cliff, and made their way into the cave. In spite of the wonders revealed by their flashlights, both were too intent on finding their chums to appreciate the cavern's beauty.

Presently they came to the point where the passage branched. While trying to decide which path to follow, they heard angry voices coming from the right fork.

"Sounds like trouble ahead," Biff whispered. "Come on!"

The boys hurried through the downwards sloping passage, which seemed endless.

Suddenly Tony grabbed Biff's arm. "Hold it!" he hissed. "Do you hear what I hear?"

Biff nodded grimly. Both recognized Chin Gok's voice. Switching off their flashlights, the two crept forward stealthily. Their jaws tightened in horror at the lamplit scene that met their eyes in the huge, subterranean chamber just ahead!

Frank, Joe and Chet were propped against the wall, their arms and legs bound with ropes. Chin Gok, Dr Montrose and the two Coast Guard impostors were standing a short distance away.

"As Butler has just informed you," Chin Gok was saying with evil relish, "all three of you will be tossed into this pool as soon as Dr Montrose and I put these securities and jewels in our pockets."

Biff and Tony clenched their fists. They must do something! There was no time to go for help. Conferring in tense whispers, they settled on a plan of action.

"It's a long shot," Tony muttered, "but it may work. We'll have to chance it." He took out his jack-knife and switched open the blade to cut the prisoners' bonds.

"Okay—*now*!"

Like sprinters taking off at a race, the two boys burst into the open! Dr Montrose and Chin Gok, who had not yet picked up the loot, were standing by the green pool. Biff and Tony let out wild war whoops and charged!

Before the startled men knew what was happening, Biff's sudden assault pushed Chin Gok head-first into the pool! Tony's hard jab toppled Dr Montrose after him.

Burns and Butler let out roars of rage. Biff, who was rangy and powerful, sent Burns sprawling and started to tackle the other.

Meanwhile, Tony had begun to slash the ropes that held the Hardys and Chet. Frank surged into action the instant he was free.

Just in time! His first punch made Butler's knees buckle as he was about to land a finishing blow on Biff.

But the fight was far from over! Burns was up and now all four tangled in a fierce slugging match. Then Joe waded in and the tide of battle began to turn.

"Quick!" Chet gasped as Tony sawed frantically at his ropes. He had just spotted Chin Gok crawling out of the pool. The enraged Chinese was dripping from head to foot with greenish slime.

A knife flashed in his right hand just as the last strands of Chet's rope parted. The chunky boy moved with unexpected rapidity. Head down, he rammed into the huge Chinese, butting him in the solar plexus. With a gurgle, Chin Gok collapsed in a heap, moaning. Chet took his knife away and threw it into the pool.

By now Butler and Burns were reeling and giving ground swiftly. Minutes later they went down, begging for mercy.

"Where's Dr Montrose?" Frank asked suddenly. "Still in the pool?"

"There he goes!" Joe cried, seeing a slimy green figure just disappearing from the cavern. "Tony! Biff! Chet! Take care of these prisoners!" he requested. "Come on, Frank! We'll get the Chameleon!"

The Hardys' chums began tying their captives with the ropes which had bound their friends a few minutes earlier. After gathering up the loot, they marched the men out of the cave and down the cliff. Dave Roberts could take charge of them until the Coast Guard sent over officers to look after the prisoners.

Meanwhile, Frank and Joe had raced after the Chameleon. Upon reaching the fork in the tunnel, the young sleuths noticed that the path they had not explored had wet footprints in it.

"That phoney doctor went this way!" Joe exclaimed, and they sped through the zigzag opening.

The tunnel was fairly short and rose sharply to the top of the cliff. The exit was so narrow, Frank and Joe had to squeeze through it. Once outside they looked for Dr Montrose. They spotted him jumping from rock to rock down the far side of the cliff.

"I see a boat down there!" Frank cried out. "He'll escape in it!"

The Hardys descended the treacherous hillside as fast as they dared but felt that the chase was hopeless. But as Montrose reached the foot of the cliff, the brothers suddenly spied Clams Dagget on the shore.

"Clams!" Frank shouted. "Grab that man! He's a thief!"

The beachcomber-pilot looked up. Recognizing the Hardys, he did not hesitate. Before the fleeing Chameleon knew what was happening, he had been tripped and thrown face down to the sand. By the time Frank and Joe reached him, Clams was seated astride the doctor's shoulders, thwarting the man's efforts to rise. When Montrose saw the Hardys, he ceased to struggle and the beachcomber let him get up.

"Now s'pose you fellows tell me what this is all about," Clams demanded.

The boys gave him an account of everything they knew, including the prime clue of the cuff links.

Clams frowned and said, "If we search this jerk, mebbe we can find out more."

Montrose objected, but Frank and Joe held him as the beachcomber began going through the man's pockets. As he looked over the contents of the doctor's wallet, Clams exclaimed:

"Quite a bunch o' dough. Hm. A hundred-dollar bill! By crickey, if there ain't two of 'em!"

"Let me see them!" Joe cried out. As soon as they were removed from the wallet he said excitedly, "Frank, these bills belong to you and me! I remember the letters and numbers. Federal reserve notes from the eighth and the fifth districts. The first starts with H18 and ends with F. That's yours. And the other, starting E1015 and ending with A, is my bill!"

The Chameleon's face went white. "You kids are smart," he growled, "but dumb sometimes. I saw you put the money in the envelope and lay it on the mantelpiece while I was casing your house preparatory to opening the safe, so I came in and took it."

"That *was* dumb of me," Joe agreed. "Well, get marching. We're going to hand you over to the Coast Guard."

As the group of four neared the bathing beach, they could see a Coast Guard craft docking next to the *Hai Hau*. Officers jumped from the boat and hurried towards the boys and their prisoners. They got further confessions from the men, including the fact that Butler and Burns were the ones who had signalled to Montrose on shore to tell him and Chin Gok when it was safe for them to visit the island cave.

"We tried to scare you guys away that night you came snoopin' around in your boat," Butler told the Hardys. "We hired two men to do it."

The brothers learned, too, that Burns had acted as Montrose's "stockbroker" friend.

Clams had been quiet up to this point. Now he burst out, "If I'd known you two was such low-downs, I'd never 'a' sold you one mouthful o' clams all those times you come pesterin' me for 'em. And you never did tell me what that job was you wanted me to do. Guess it was somethin' crooked and you found out I'm an honest guy!"

With the Coast Guard in charge of the prisoners and the loot, the Hardys and their pals said goodbye to Clams and headed for the *Hai Hau*. Biff now revealed the news about the finding of the treasure map.

"Wow-ee!" Joe cried out and hugged Tony exuberantly.

Frank followed, grinning from ear to ear. "Super!" he exclaimed. "Say, look who's coming!"

At this moment Ti-Ming, evidently waiting for the boys, walked forward to add his congratulations on the capture of the two slick thieves and their pals. He said he had come to the island in a private launch to tell the boys that Chief Collig and his men had caught the other Chinese who had escaped from jail with Chin Gok.

Upon hearing of the finding of the scroll, he remarked, "Very fine work! The whole gang in custody, and the mystery of the Chinese junk solved! I came prepared to search and help. Instead, all I can do is offer you a reward."

"Reward?" the boys chorused.

Ti-Ming smiled. "The rightful owner of the *Hai Hau* instructed me to tell the finder of the clue to the fortune that he would receive a ten per cent interest in it."

"Guess you're elected, Tony," said Frank.

"Hope you make a million," Joe added.

Tony Prito reddened, then said, "Anything that comes to Bayport from those mines of blue amber will be shared, and shared in equal amounts, among the six of us. We all bought the *Hai Hau* together, didn't we?"

Ti-Ming beamed with pleasure. "And you solved the mystery together. Now I must leave, but first I apologize for the telegram about the curse to keep you from selling the *Hai Hau*."

As they waved goodbye to George Ti-Ming, Frank and Joe wondered what new mystery would rise up to challenge them.

Frank went aboard the *Hai Hau* and rang the junk's melodic bell, calling the picnickers aboard.

"It's a little early," Frank confessed to his pals, "but I want to be at the airport when Mother and Dad arrive."

"Yes," said Joe. "And what a home-coming they're going to get!"